T H E
DALLERGUT
DREAM-
MAKING
DISTRICT

THE DALLERGUT DREAM-MAKING DISTRICT

A Novel

MIYE LEE

TRANSLATED BY SANDY JOOSUN LEE

HANOVER
SQUARE
PRESS

HANOVER
SQUARE
PRESS™

Recycling programs
for this product may
not exist in your area.

ISBN-13: 978-1-335-01535-8

The Dallergut Dream-Making District

Originally published in South Korea as 달러구트 꿈 백화점 2 – 단골손님을 찾습니다 by Sam & Parkers Co., Ltd. in 2021.

First published in the English language in 2024 by Wildfire, an imprint of Headline Publishing Group, in arrangement with Sam & Parkers Co., Ltd. c/o KCC (Korea Copyright Center Inc.), Seoul, and Chiara Tognetti Rights Agency, Milan.

This English edition was published by Harlequin Enterprises ULC, 2025, by arrangement with Sam & Parkers Co., Ltd. c/o KCC (Korea Copyright Center Inc.), Seoul, and Chiara Tognetti Rights Agency, Milan.

Hanover Square Press
22 Adelaide St. West, 41st Floor
Toronto, Ontario M5H 4E3, Canada
HanoverSqPress.com

Printed in U.S.A.

Also by Miye Lee

The Dallergut Dream Department Store

PROLOGUE
DALLERGUT'S ATTIC

The night is deep, but Penny and her parents are wide awake. They live together about a mile south of the Dallergut Dream Department Store, where Penny works at the front desk. Tonight, they're having a late-night dinner to celebrate her first work anniversary.

"You've adapted to the job so well over the past year. I'm so proud of you, Penny. This is our gift for our baby girl." Penny's dad wrestles with a stack of books tied with twine, trying to put them on the dining table. They are all self-help books and essay collections tailored to those just starting out in their careers.

"Well, I don't know if I'll have time to read all these, unless my day magically extends to forty-eight hours," Penny says, untying the twine ribbon. "I do have good news. After a year at the department store, I'm officially a government-approved member of the dream industry!"

"Oh! Does that mean . . . ?"

"Yes! They'll give me a pass to the Company District in the west. I'll be having a one-on-one salary negotiation tomorrow. Maybe that's when Dallergut will hand me the pass! I think it's finally sinking in that I work at the dream department store."

"Look at you. I've been jealous of people commuting to the Company District all my life, and my own daughter's going to be one of them . . ." Penny's dad looks at her, his eyes brimming with emotion. She has her father's eyes.

"Well, I think it's much more impressive to work at the department store than in the Company District," Penny's mom chimes in, wiping some cream sauce from her lips. "So, what will you be doing in the district?"

"I'm not sure. Maybe meeting with the dreammakers as part of our off-site work? I've been there to see Yasnoozz Otra at her mansion. There are a lot of dreammakers and production studios, so maybe I'll run errands here and there."

Penny recalls visiting Yasnoozz Otra, one of the Legendary Big Five, to pick up her dream, "Lives of Others (Trial Version)."

"Can't believe our baby girl is all grown-up now . . . But stay out of trouble this time, okay?"

"Yes, my dear. No more big mistakes like last year. Always stay on your toes."

Penny nods, her stomach beginning to twist. Her parents have been nagging her more often lately. It all started when the police called, and her mom happened to pick up the phone. They were looking to verify the suspect behind a stolen Flutter bottle, and Penny had no choice but to share the details of how her Flutter had been stolen at the bank. Ever since then, her parents' pestering has been so intense that her ears hurt, and she's made a mental note that she should never share what happens at work with her parents.

Tonight, Penny endures another relentless storm of nagging. She offers familiar assurances like, "Don't worry, Dad," and "I said I'm not that stupid, Mom." By the time she finishes her meal, she feels exhausted.

"You two enjoy the rest of your dinner. I'm heading back to my room."

Penny dumps the stack of books onto her desk. Her bookcase has no room for these new additions. She contemplates for a moment, then pulls out the practice test workbooks she once used when applying for jobs.

"It's time to go, guys," says Penny resolutely, bidding farewell to her old books.

Penny opens one of the test-prep books she never finished. If her answers were erasable, she could resell it, but all the questions have been underlined with bold pen strokes. Disappointed, she flips through the pages until her eyes reach the last question she solved. Her furry, big-clawed Noctiluca friend Assam had helped her with the question when she was preparing for the department store interview on the second floor of her favorite café.

Q. Which dream and dreammaker won the Grand Prix at the 1999 Dream of the Year Awards by a unanimous vote?

  a. "Crossing the Pacific Ocean as a Killer Whale" by Kick Slumber

  b. "Living as My Parents for a Week" by Yasnoozz Otra

  c. "Floating in Space Gazing Down on Earth" by Wawa Sleepland

  d. "Teatime with a Historical Figure" by Doje

  e. "An Infertile Couple's Dream Foretelling the Birth of Triplets" by Babynap Rockabye

The question instantly transports Penny back to a year ago. She perfectly recalls the answer.

"It's *a*—Kick Slumber's debut work at age thirteen," mutters Penny with a confident smile, placing the book back down with a thud.

Thinking of that day at the café, prepping for the interview, the events of the past year flash through Penny's mind. She basks in the deep sense of achievement from the most fulfilling year of her life. Now, she feels adept at her front-desk job, more confident than ever, and enriched with valuable lessons and experiences.

Penny organizes her bookcase, humming to herself, blissfully oblivious. Little does she know that she's merely scratched the surface of what truly transpires at the dream store. With excitement and a bit of trepidation, the night of her work anniversary comes to a close.

* * *

Dallergut finds himself in the comfort of his attic room, situated atop the department store he proudly owns, a deluxe wooden building that hosts an array of dreams on each floor.

The attic is secretly tucked away above the discount section of the fifth floor. From outside the building, it doesn't look much like a place to live, with its pointed triangular roof and tiny windows. Inside, it turns out to be much more spacious, but it's still a modest residence for someone of Dallergut's celebrated reputation. People often ask if he ever dreams of living in a luxurious mansion like the famous dreammakers or the other big store owners, but Dallergut does not intend to leave the cozy attic, which he has decorated to reflect his tastes and interests. More than anything, he quite enjoys the commute to his office on the first floor, which takes him less than three minutes.

The attic is uniquely arranged with four beds in the center. Their headboards face each other, each with a different bedframe, mattress height and bedding material. A custom-made canopy gracefully descends from the ceiling, enveloping the four beds so that whichever bed he sleeps in feels equally comfortable and open.

The unique setup allows Dallergut to choose a different bed based on the mood and dream he wants to experience each night. It was, without a doubt, the biggest investment of his modest life. By contrast, everything else in his room appears to have been left unattended and neglected. The aging cabinetry has started to warp, making it challenging to open its doors. After repeated haphazard fixes, most of the appliances don't work well. The faded paint has long been peeling from the stained window frames. Even the sensor in front of the attic door turns on and off erratically. But Dallergut remains indifferent.

Earlier this evening, Dallergut had left work early and come to find solace in his attic. Now, clad in his pajamas, he sits on the edge of the lowest bed, engrossed in a stack of more than thirty letters that have arrived throughout the week. Some lie open and scattered across the bed.

**The Biggest Young Minds of the
Company District Join Forces!**

"Duo Dream" by Researcher-Turned-
Dreammakers Currently in Development

"Sleep Tight. See You in My Dream" Becomes
a Literal Reality!

Dear Mr. Dallergut,
We are honored to offer you the exclusive sales
rights to our newest title . . .

The Dallergut Dream Department Store is always flooded
with exclusive offers for newly released dream products.
Dreammakers send letters to Dallergut even before their
dream is complete, hoping to leverage the prospect of a
deal with the prestigious Dallergut to attract potential in-
vestors. But Dallergut knows better than anyone that such
dreams usually end up stuck in development.

Bored, he rips open the last letter. When he realizes
that this is the letter he's been eagerly waiting for, his
face lights up.

Dear Mr. Dallergut,
Thank you for the event pitch deck. We are very
intrigued and would be delighted to join.
   Our team will soon forward a list of items we can
sponsor.
Sincerely,
Bedtown Furniture

This event, which Dallergut considers the biggest
event he's ever held, has been his sole focus lately. Set to
take place in the fall, it is an ambitious plan he has not
yet shared with his employees.

Fortunately, he has been receiving positive responses
from potential corporate sponsors. At this rate, things
may take shape soon, and he may even be able share the
exciting news with his staff in a few months.

After reading the last letter from Bedtown Furniture,
Dallergut stands up to stretch his back. He can't bring
himself to clean up all the letters strewn across the bed.

"When will it get easier to organize . . . ? Well, I'll do
a mass cleanup over the weekend."

He puts off cleaning and stands in front of the bookcase that he had custom-made to cover the entire side
wall, looking for something light to read before sleeping. At eye level are a series of yearly journals, organized
chronologically.

"Oh yes, I should read our customers' journals before
the event. Should come in quite handy."

He selects one. The journal is an old-fashioned bundle
of loose sheets bound together with a coarse string. The
cover is made of thick, rough cardboard, stained with
time. A title scrawled carefully on the cover in black ink
reads *Dream Journal, 1999* in Dallergut's own handwriting. He has always loved crafts and calligraphy, anything

handmade. By comparison, he struggles with anything even slightly technological. Everyone at the Dallergut Dream Department Store knows that he does not pair well with machines, even simple ones like printers.

Dallergut slips under the blanket of the bed closest to the entrance, holding the worn-out journal. The fluffy texture of the bedding embraces him from head to toe. But before he has flipped through more a few pages, drowsiness overtakes him. He rubs the corners of his eyes with his long fingers, trying to fight sleep, but his body keeps conceding. He's spent all his energy today doing the legwork for his big secret event, on top of the usual tasks in the store.

"I miss the good old days when I used to have infinite energy . . ." Dallergut sighs, which turns into a yawn as his eyes water. A good night's sleep is a much better option right now. He has a packed schedule tomorrow with one-on-one salary negotiations.

Deciding to catch up on the journal later, Dallergut places it on his round bedside table, leaving the pages wide open so he can continue where he left off. With a gentle tug of the light switch's long string, he turns it off and falls asleep as soon as his head hits the pillow.

Now the only sounds in the dark attic are those of Dallergut's low, deep breaths and the steady ticking of the clock. The faint moonlight from the window spills into every corner of the room, and a breeze comes through the cracks in the glass. Just then, the broken sensor light by the entrance flickers on. Its crimson glow clashes with the moonlight from the window, shining like a spotlight on the very part of the journal that Dallergut left unread.

August 20th, 1999

Just woke up from a dream and I feel like I should write everything down before this vivid sensation disappears.

In the dream, I was a gigantic killer whale. I was heading farther and farther from shore, out into the vast sea. The salty water rushing through my nose in painful, gasping breaths, the fear of being caught in waves and not making it out alive . . . these were not my main concerns. I'm most impressed by the overwhelmingly immersive nature of the dream.

Kick Slumber's dream offers freedom, not the precarious kind that leaves you without footing, but that feeling of safety we all desire. The deeper the sea, the more I felt like I was at home, in my elements.

I felt the muscles running from my dorsal fin to my tail. I slammed the tail down hard and lifted it back up, instantly picking up speed. The surface of the water was now the ceiling of my world, unfolding from beneath my white belly, and my world was deeper than the sky.

I could see, although I didn't need to. I could already feel the world with my other senses. I leaped to the surface on impulse. The word *impossible* never crossed my mind. My perfect hydrodynamic body breached the surface of the ocean and soared valiantly, cutting through the air.

Suddenly, a tingling sensation swept through my body, one I wasn't sure belonged to me. I started to worry about my previous self that I had left at the shore. I tried to continue swimming, releasing my thoughts into the roaring waves.

"This is where I belong."

As I grew used to the heightened senses, I began to wonder if I had been a killer whale all along. Then, I came to a state where I was neither a killer whale nor a human, where the worlds overlapped and separated from each other. That's when I woke up from the dream.

It feels like an inevitable destiny that I dreamed of the debut work of the thirteen-year-old Kick Slumber at this moment and time. This genius boy may well become the youngest Grand Prix winner this year.

But I guess I will never witness that myself . . .
Anything more than this would be too dangerous . . .

That is all that is written on that page. Just then, the broken sensor light goes out, and darkness descends on the attic once again.

The unknown dreamer's entry in the open journal,

along with Dallergut's old furniture and all his clutter, creates an eerie atmosphere. It stands in stark contrast to the dream department store downstairs, bright and lively twenty-four seven, with customers stopping by to do their dream-shopping.

ONE

PENNY'S FIRST SALARY NEGOTIATION

Days have flown by since the New Year, and it is now the last Friday of March. The savory scent of simmering onion milk from the food truck floats through the cool evening breeze, permeating every little street corner. The comforting smell reminds dream-shoppers of relaxing underneath a warm blanket with only their heads poking out into the cool air.

The Dallergut Dream Department Store lobby is still buzzing with customers. The night-shift employees start arriving, but Penny, now a second-year employee at the front desk, is in the staff lounge located on the right side of the entrance, waiting for her turn to negotiate her salary.

With a sturdy push, the arched door swings open, revealing the staff lounge. Penny sits with a few other employees, including her old friend from school, Motail, who works on the fifth floor. Despite its modest size, the lounge is a treasured haven for employees.

The unique yellow lighting, the cushions with loose stitches, the low humming of someone talking, the sound of someone pulling up a chair, and the gentle whirring of the small refrigerator and copy machine. It all feels like home. To Penny, the lounge is like a clubhouse or the common rooms where she used to spend the bulk of her time during college.

Perched on an armchair, Penny turns to Motail, who's sitting next to her. "Is it our turn soon?" she asks.

"After Myers is Speedo, then me, then you. We're almost there."

"Thought it would be over by the end of our shift. It's a little past that now."

Penny stretches overhead, glancing at the clock on the wall.

"Well, you know Dallergut's always busy, and today is no exception. He seems especially swamped these days. I would've picked up some toast from Kirk Barrier's Bakery had I known it would run this late." Motail clucks, patting the round belly that protrudes from beneath his snug sweater.

Still, they sit patiently, waiting their turn, because salary negotiations only come around once a year. This marks Penny's first. She shrugs her shoulders with pride, relishing the feeling of being a true grown-up, but she doesn't actually expect a raise.

It was around this time a year ago when the Flutter bottle incident happened. Penny is still reeling from it, but the culprit was caught recently, and the stolen bottle has been confiscated. She was overjoyed by the news at first, but then when she learned that Speedo was the one who had caught the culprit, she's had to endure his smug *You're welcome* look every time she runs into him. Still, it's a big relief that a potentially unfavorable factor in her salary negotiation has been removed. Regardless, she doesn't feel the need to ask for more.

Under a rustic chandelier dotted with crystals sit Summer and her manager Mogberry. Like her colleagues on the third floor, Summer wears a personalized work apron—a creation of her own, one hem loose and hanging longer than others. Across from Summer, Mogberry's cheeks glow with a thick layer of blush. This was probably an attempt to mask her natural flush during the negotiation, yet it only draws more attention to her under the warm yellow light. Having already concluded their salary negotiation, the two munch on snacks, showing no intentions of leaving the lounge any time soon. The large snack basket, which at the start of the day was filled with luxurious treats like Calm Cookies, now holds only a handful of plain coin-shaped chocolates.

Summer has laid out a set of cards on the wooden table for a personality test and has been posing a series of questions to Mogberry.

"Now, let's see what we've got! Mogberry, you are a Passionate Campaigner! A *First Disciple* type. This is the third time you've got the same result."

Mogberry's eyes twinkle. She nods passionately, clearly satisfied with the result. "I should do it again and see if I get it a fourth time!"

Summer twitches her long nose, visibly uncomfortable.

The personality cards are inspired by the story of *The Time God and the Three Disciples*, and the idea is to match people with whichever one of the three disciples' personalities that they most resemble. It started out as a bookstore's beginning-of-the-year freebie with any purchase over ten gordens. But its design sparked an appetite for collecting, causing a shortage. Penny has been eager to get her hands on a set of her own through a secondhand marketplace; she even considered paying a premium for it.

"Motail, care to try out the test?" asks Summer, spreading the cards again. She seems to be growing tired of dealing with only Mogberry.

"No, thanks. I'm sure mine will be the *First Disciple* type anyway. I consider myself to be forward-thinking,"

Motail responds cheerfully, as he sweeps up the last of the chocolates from the basket, handing some to Penny before he sits back down. "Penny, you said you live with your parents, right? Don't you need to give them a call and let them know you're coming home late?" he asks, peeling off the silver wrapper of the chocolate.

"I already did. I told them to eat dinner without me."

Penny doesn't mind the idea of spending extra time in the staff lounge after work. She is excited to swing by the deli on her way home and grab a fat chicken-no-veggie sandwich to eat while watching a late-night TV series. There's no rush for her to get home early, especially when it means avoiding the barrage of questions from her parents about how her salary negotiation went, whether she was scolded by the boss, or if she did anything wrong with the customers.

Minutes later, the wooden arched door barks open. Penny assumes it's Vigo Myers, coming to call out the next name after his own meeting wrapped up quickly. To her surprise, it's Speedo.

Speedo is the manager of the fourth floor, which showcases dreams for when you're napping. He's a high performer with a quick temper and a long ponytail. Dressed in the same jumpsuit he wears all year round, he holds several thick files as he scopes out the people in the lounge.

"Myers not done yet?"

"No, I think it'll take a while," Penny answers reflexively, but instantly regrets drawing Speedo's attention.

"Oh, Penny. Am I making you jumpy? I know you're utterly grateful that I caught the Flutter culprit for you . . ."

"No, I'm fine."

Speedo plops down on the edge of the couch, giving Penny a generous look that says *I know you're too embarrassed to admit that I make you nervous.*

"By the way, Mogberry, how did the renovation go?" asks Penny, changing the topic after giving Speedo an awkward smile in response. "You said you put extra care into the windows."

Until recently, Mogberry has been commuting to work from her sister's house while her own home gets renovated. Her sister happens to live near Penny, and the two have often bumped into each other on their commute. Mogberry mentioned the other day that the renovation was complete.

"Oh, you remember! That's right. I love my new windows! I took a big leap of faith and made them extra wide. I can see all the way to the Dizzying Downhill to the west! Such a nice view. Especially when the weather's good."

"Then, you must also see the train going in and out of the Company District! Amazing!"

"That's exactly why I wanted it. I'll be lazing around the house on my days off, watching people go to work in the Company District, which doubles the fun," Mogberry responds excitedly, almost as if she's been waiting for Penny to ask. Taking advantage of this distraction, Summer starts packing the personality test cards into their case, seeming grateful that Mogberry's attention has waned from them.

From the main street where the Dallergut Dream Department Store and numerous shops are located, the large residential area in which Penny lives extends to the south. To the north soars the Million-Year Snow Mountain, home to Nicholas, famously known as Santa Claus. In the east, an upscale neighborhood accommodates celebrities like Yasnoozz Otra, along with their personal dream production studios. Lastly, to the west lies the Dizzying Downhill, infamous for its sheer, dizzying drop.

Descending into a valley and then ascending a steep climb to the west sprawls a vast area where large dream production studios operate. They call it the Company District.

The route to the district is too rugged for cars or subways, and taking a detour around the challenging terrain would make the journey exceptionally longer. Typically, the Company District workers take the exclusive express commuter train, which goes back and forth to the district dozens of times a day, moving along rails laid uphill and downhill.

"Hey, Penny and Motail, you've never been on the train before, right?" Mogberry asks.

"Actually, I have," Motail rebuts. "Once. I heard they don't really check passes for out-of-town guests in pajamas, so I took a test ride in pajamas with my friends from the neighborhood, just to see. It only lasted about ten seconds before I got caught by the train driver."

The commuter train to the Company District is not for the public. You need to have a form of identification to prove that you work in the dream industry, like a district employee ID card or a dreammaker's license. Even employees at the Dallergut Dream Department Store have to work for over a year to get the pass.

"But haven't you been working at the dream store for more than a year now?" Summer asks Motail, neatly arranging all the cards back in their case.

"Yes, my first work anniversary was last summer. But the pass is distributed to everyone in March, so I had to wait until now. Penny, you said you barely turned one year just in time?"

"Yes, as of yesterday. I was lucky. If I'd been hired a day later, I would have had to wait another year." Penny places a hand to her chest with a short sigh of relief.

"Looks like these kids are finally going to get a taste of the infamous Civil Complaint Center." Speedo, who has been quiet, suddenly chimes in. He's been shaking his legs nervously, flipping through his files at a frightening pace.

"Oh, stop those legs—and that nonsense," Mogberry scolds him.

"Nonsense? Mogberry, you know what it means to have a pass to the district. This is not for a joyride or a field trip to the dream production studios."

"Of course I know that. But it doesn't have to be that serious."

"It's not a joyride or a field trip to production studios?" Motail seems shocked.

"You're too optimistic, kid. Speedo's right. Your pass is mainly for the Civil Complaint Center, located in the Company District Central Square."

"We're not allowed to go inside the production studios, then?" Motail wraps his hands around his head in despair.

"Of course not! The only places you're allowed are the Civil Complaint Center and maybe the Test Center upstairs, period. That's where we have painful meetings with the dreammakers to address complaints that come in."

"What is the Civil Complaint Center?" Penny asks.

"Better to see it for yourself than hear about it from

us. I vividly remember the first time I followed Dallergut to the center. It's a place you can't avoid if you're in
the dream business, but it's a place you *want* to avoid if
you can help it . . . Well . . . It's an uncomfortable place."
The corners of Mogberry's eyes droop sullenly.

"The customers you kids have seen are all smiles, but
wait until you see the complaints coming into the center. You'll realize, yet again, how great this Speedo is.
Just look at all these complaints I had to resolve for the
nap dreams I sold last year!" Speedo compliments himself and gestures at his hefty stack of files.

"Speedo, did you compile a whole year's worth of
complaints as leverage for the salary negotiation with
Dallergut?" Mogberry's jaw drops in surprise.

"That's correct, Mogberry. I printed all of them out
and put them in a binder so Dallergut could see just
how much work I put into it. Want to see how many of
these are plain absurd? I can understand a complaint like
*My classmate made fun of me for sleep-talking while dreaming
in class.* What I don't get is a complaint like *I can't sleep
at night because a dream I had during the nap was so much
fun that I overslept until the evening.* I mean, what do you
want me to do? They have no idea how many nights I've
spent dealing with this . . ."

"And all those hours and devoted hard work led you
to becoming the manager of the fourth floor, isn't that

right? Not everyone gets to be named a floor manager at the Dallergut Dream Department Store. That's an incredible step for your career," says Summer, cupping her chin in her hands, with a hint of both admiration and jealousy in her voice.

Penny can barely understand half of what Speedo is saying in his stream of rapid-fire speech, but what she knows is that he's probably the only one who can handle that much work.

"I bet the salary negotiation will literally be a negotiation for you floor managers. You guys seem so far away from us. And here I was, ready to just say yes and sign off on whatever Dallergut offers." Penny suddenly feels overwhelmed by the thought of the meeting, knowing her turn is close.

"Don't worry. Dallergut wouldn't expect much from a one-year-old newbie like yourself. Instead, he'll be curious about your plans for this year." Summer comforts Penny.

"My plans . . . Can *Doing my best at what I'm doing now* be considered a plan? You know, like guiding the customers at the front desk, managing the inventories, and doing what Weather asks me to do. Besides completing those duties, I've never given much thought to anything else."

"That's a wonderful plan in and of itself. But won't

you get bored? I'd go stir-crazy if I had to complete the same tasks in the same spot of the store every single day," says Motail, his back stiffening at the thought.

"But you don't seem bored at all working on the fifth floor."

Motail is notorious for being the most boisterous dreamseller in the discount section. He bounces around, sometimes frightening customers out of their wits, spewing his sales pitches incessantly. But even Penny wants to purchase a discounted dream immediately when she sees Motail in action.

"Motail, do you have a plan about what to leverage in your salary negotiation?"

"Yes, I do. A grand one, indeed."

"Like what?"

"In my opinion . . . It's time the fifth floor had its own manager." Motail lowers his voice as he leans fully into the armrest of Penny's chair, lest anyone else hear him. "Look at Mogberry. She is young, but she's already a manager. Maybe I can be fifth-floor manager one day. As you know, I have quite a knack for picking out good products. And while it might be premature to reveal my ambition already, maybe someday . . ." Motail clenches his fist confidently, like a kid performing at a speech contest.

Motail's words are not a bluff. He does have an eye

for identifying products that would sell well. The new releases he recommends may not be huge hits, but they perform well enough to consistently run out of stock. At the end of the year, when Dallergut gifted the employees with coupons for whatever dream they liked, there was a saying among them: *If you don't know which dream to pick, pick the one Motail picks.*

"You're right. You do have a keen eye for good products."

Penny is mildly shocked by Motail's ambition, but she tries to cover it up with a compliment. Seeing a coworker of the same age planning to get ahead is a source of both anxiety and motivation.

Why hadn't I realized this before?

Penny has vaguely assumed that this year will be the same as last year. But she can't just do what her boss Weather, the first-floor manager, tells her to do forever. She can no longer expect a grace period as a new hire, assuming that things will effortlessly fall into place. The realization hits her that she might lag far behind others who have plans of their own, like Motail. Her mouth goes dry, her initial excitement about the pass to the Company District giving way to a harsher reality.

The lounge door opens again, and this time, it actually is Vigo Myers. The manager of the "Daily" section on the second floor, Myers always wears a stoic expression, so his salary negotiation outcome remains a mystery to everyone.

"Your turn," says Myers to Speedo, who marches off to Dallergut's office with his thick stack of files, resolute. Myers is about to follow him out when Mogberry stops him.

"Hey, Myers, you should also try the personality test! It tells you which of the three disciples you are most like. I'm curious which type you are." Mogberry casually pulls the cards back out of the case.

"Not interested. You know there can't be just three types of people," Myers responds apathetically.

"Don't be stubborn. It's just for fun. Then, how about you, Penny?"

"Me? Yes. Sure." Penny has been lost in thought and answers before she realizes what she has agreed to.

Excited, Mogberry moves closer to Penny and lays out the cards on the table. A total of twenty-five cards are presented in rows of five, each with a different, beautiful decoration. The corners of the cards have design elements that connect with the cards laid out diagonally from them. You pick up a card based on your answers to each question and stack them on top of one another. The last card you end up with will determine your personality type.

"At least they made it look nice," Myers says, in contrast to his former lack of interest. Instead of leaving the room, he stands behind Penny, glancing at the cards.

"Now, shall we start? After you answer all my questions, you will end up with one of these three cards." Mogberry repeats the lines she had heard Summer say quite a few times and points to three colorful, translucent cards placed in the bottom row.

The leftmost card features the back of an old woman reaching for a radiant light, interlaced with dangling fruits, which is toward the card's border. The woman clearly represents Babynap Rockabye, the dreammaker of conception dreams.

The middle card has tiny crystals sparkling like stars in a dark, cavelike place, with a tiny man reaching for one of the sparkles. The third card shows a man who's the spitting image of Dallergut, standing in front of the dream department store.

Just when Penny is about to ask who the second card represents, Mogberry picks it up and flips it over so Penny can't see the painting.

Mogberry starts the test, holding a sheet of questions.

"Do you often find yourself lost in the past when you're alone?"

"Um . . . Yes, that tends to happen."

"Do you believe your past has a significant impact on you?"

At the second question, Penny is reminded of Spee-do's discomfiting smile, which has been bothering her lately. "Yes."

"Okay. Do you find joy in exploring new things rather than settling into a daily routine?"

"No . . . I don't think so."

With each question Penny answers, the cards that were once spread out begin to coalesce into one. Eventually, Penny finishes answering the last question, and Mogberry slowly turns over the last remaining card.

"You are . . . a gentle thinker! A *Second Disciple* type. The first among us!"

Penny takes the card from Mogberry's hand and examines it closely. Along the top border of the picture is a small passage from *The Time God and the Three Disciples*. Penny knows it well.

The Second Disciple believed that holding on to the memories would make them forever happy without remorse or emptiness. The Time God granted the Second Disciple the past with the power to forever cherish all old memories.

"By the way, who are the Second Disciple's descendants?" Penny asks what has been on her mind throughout the test. "The story says they hid deep in the caves. No one knows what happened to them afterward?"

"Well, it's more like no one these days is interested in finding out. It's ancient history. And you only discovered last year that Babynap Rockabye is the descendant of the First Disciple. Everyone knows Dallergut is the descendant of the Third Disciple, but that's only because the dream department store has been passed down for generations. Rumor has it that the Second Disciple's descendants are making dreams in secret—or that they have all died out. But I'm not so sure."

"Atlas," Myers spits out as soon as Mogberry finishes.

"I'm sorry?" Penny asks.

"The name's Atlas. The descendant of the Second Disciple," Myers blurts brusquely, then yanks the door open. "Well, I'd better get going. You guys should, too. Don't bother sticking around here. If you're done, go home."

Just as Myers leaves, Speedo comes rushing in, his salary negotiation complete. His meeting was as quick as a restroom break. Motail, who is next in line, stumbles out of his seat for his own meeting.

Shortly after, Penny leaves the lounge herself and paces in front of Dallergut's office, waiting for her turn. The lobby is full of out-of-town customers in pajamas, some of them stopping by on their way home from work.

Penny's personality test results float around in her mind like dust motes. Motail would have got the future-minded *First Disciple* type. *If his goal-orientated and driven traits are inherent, what are my strengths as a* Second Disciple *type? How can the Second Disciple's ability to "cherish any memory for a long time" be useful?* Penny wonders. All that comes to mind is how it might help in a memorization-heavy exam. Penny agrees with Myers that people can't be categorized into just three types, but her mind keeps wandering. In fact, she gets so lost in thought that she doesn't notice the door opening. Motail has come out from his salary negotiation, and looks puzzled to find Penny in a daze by the door.

"Penny, you okay?"

"Oh, you're done. Yeah, I'm good."

"Well, then. Go ahead." Motail gently holds open the door for her. He seems to be in a good mood. His salary negotiation must have gone well.

"Thanks, Motail."

Penny walks into the office, where Dallergut greets her with a wave. He's sitting behind his desk, wearing a black-and-white knitted sweater, which bears a striking semblance to his semicurly, grizzled hair.

"Sorry to keep you waiting for so long. Please, have a seat."

"No worries, Dallergut."

Dallergut dons a pair of thin-rimmed reading glasses. He looks more insightful with the glasses on. Despite his impeccable appearance, his office resembles his more modest, down-to-earth side. The troublesome old printer is flashing its red light, and the large desk is cluttered with bundles of paper waiting for Dallergut's approval, old diaries turned upside down, and bottles of unfinished drinks.

"Some people find comfort in a little bit of clutter," Dallergut says nonchalantly, as if he can read what's on Penny's mind. "I don't suppose you'll need a Calm Cookie today?"

"Of course not." Penny smiles, calm in pretense.

"So here we are. The first salary negotiation for you, as an employee for the front desk on the first floor. Shall we take a look back at last year?"

Dallergut starts searching his desk for a piece of paper that must have Penny's information. As he pulls it out from under the pencil holder, he elbows one of the leftover beverage bottles and nearly knocks it over. Luckily, Penny, who was watching the bottle anxiously, quickly catches it before it tips over. She picks up the old diary with her other hand, saving it from nearly being soaked.

"Thanks, Penny."

"You're welcome."

Penny puts the diary back on the desk. The front cover reads *Dream Journal, 1999*. She recognizes the now-familiar handwriting.

"*Dream Journal, 1999* . . . This is your handwriting. Do you keep a dream journal, Dallergut?"

"Oh, no, it's not my journal. I just made a cover for it

to look like one. I wanted to keep a record of the dream journal entries the out-of-town customers wrote after they woke up. I've been meaning to read it in my downtime, but I still haven't had the chance." Dallergut smiles as he nudges the journal with the tip of his index finger.

"The outside customers keep dream journals?"

"You know how Dream Pay Systems allows you to see short reviews from the customers? This would be an exceptionally long and detailed version."

"Keeping a journal about your dreams . . . How amazing! But it wouldn't be easy for an ordinary customer to remember their dreams."

"Yes. It seems as soon as they wake up, they jot down anything they can possibly remember before the memory fades. But it's rare, and that is what makes these dream journals so precious—and why we collect them every year like this. I don't think there's anything more valuable for people like us, working directly with customers."

Penny wonders what kind of dream journal entries the customers might have left back in 1999. But Dallergut quickly tucks it away in the desk drawer.

"Sorry about the tangent. We should be talking about you today, not the customers."

Dallergut picks up the paper full of scribbles and begins to pore over it. Penny swallows hard, nervous about how he'll evaluate her performance.

"Let's see. Weather says you're quite dependable. Muth from the evening shift also shared with me that he loves your efficiency. And there's nothing more important than the opinions of the colleagues working closest to you."

Penny, relieved, silently thanks Weather and Muth.

"Oh, I have something for you."

Dallergut rummages through his bottom desk drawer and hands her a lanyard with a small badge.

"Dallergut, this is . . ."

The badge has a unique texture that gently shimmers. Engraved on its surface is the clear inscription *The Dallergut Dream Department Store—Penny*.

"It's the pass to the Company District. You applied for one on my behalf, Dallergut. Thank you!"

"Of course! You have been working with us for exactly a year already. You're now eligible to access the Company District. You're officially a valuable asset in the dream industry."

"I heard that with the pass, we're to go to the Civil Complaint Center."

"Ah, so you already know. Yes, it's a requirement for employees who have made it through the year. An educational exercise, if you will, crafted by me. I want you to come with me this coming Monday."

"Is that where people who're aren't satisfied with

their dreams go to file complaints? That's what Speedo made it sound like."

"Yes, in short. Now, I have a question for you, Penny. Should we focus on attracting new customers, or on reengaging former regulars who have stopped coming? Which do you think is more important for our store to thrive?"

"Well . . . I think engaging new customers is important . . . same as bringing back the regulars . . . But if we must choose one over the other . . ." Penny stammers.

Dallergut does occasionally catch Penny off guard with surprise questions like this, and whenever he does, his dark brown eyes spark.

"For me, it would be our regulars," she says eventually. "Maybe working at the front desk has made me attached to their Eyelid Scales. It feels like I'm with them when I'm working."

Penny especially loves the smooth eyelash movement from their scales, and their distinctive clinking sound. And when their pendulum shifts to REM sleep state, nothing beats the joy of seeing the customer walk through the store entrance.

"Me too. So it's a serious concern when our regulars, who have loved our dreams so much, suddenly stop coming. Some of them are reticent, so instead of voicing their complaints and making everyone aware, they choose not to say anything and simply never come back. I'd rather have them come to complain and ask for a refund."

Penny remembers the group of customers who asked for a refund after purchasing Maxim's trauma-transcendence dream. Dallergut had talked with them in the complaint filing room, which sits below the office they're currently in.

"That is where the Civil Complaint Center comes in. Even out-of-town customers who often forget their dreams eventually head to the center when their complaints pile up. It's more comfortable for them to reach out to a third party rather than directly to the dream store. The center manages everything in a database to analyze and share with the respective shops and dream-makers. Reviewing the complaints and addressing them properly are among the hardest tasks for me and my floor managers."

"Why would they have issues when for them, it's deferred payment? They have nothing to lose either way." Penny doesn't understand.

"I think that's what you'll need to learn this year. Many people do not want to dream for reasons they don't fully understand. If the customers don't come to claim their reserved dreams because they put off sleep, their *no-show* reflects their carelessness. But if customers end up at the Civil Complaint Center, that reflects our own carelessness. Take your time to figure it out. I'm sure you understand by now that I don't give away all the answers, since that won't benefit your learning."

"Yes, but . . . Is it at all possible to get our regulars back?" Penny tries to come off relaxed, but deep down, she's still anxious. In her own case, it's rare for her to return to a shop once she has left for good.

"Each customer is dealing with a different situation. If you remember that, it's not entirely impossible."

"I hope I can help in some way. I want to bring them back, even if it's just one."

"Is that your goal for this year?"

"Well . . . I kind of thought of it just now, but I mean it. I hope our store can keep attracting more customers. You have no idea how much I love this place."

"That means your goal is the same as mine."

"So, what are you planning to do, Dallergut?"

"Let's see . . . There is one thing I've been planning on my own. It's not set in stone, so I'm not ready to share it just yet. There's still a lot to sort out."

"It must be something special! Can I at least get a hint?"

"Well, it will be a fun event that not only I but also all the customers will enjoy. That is for sure."

"Really?"

"Now, let's go back to our topic. Oh no, it's already past work hours! Let's wrap up our negotiation so I can eat dinner. A nice meal after a hard day's work is what it

takes, you know. Let's see . . . Here is what I would like
to offer for your salary increase. How does this sound?"

Dallergut writes down a number on the salary contract with a fountain pen and hands it to Penny. She
finds the figure more generous than expected, and she
has to work hard to keep the corners of her mouth from
turning up. Dallergut has apparently taken into account
his expectations for her future potential, and reflected
this in her salary increase.

"Penny, the money we earn is for the priceless emotions of our customers. Always remember the weight of
this," Dallergut advises as Penny signs the contract.

"Yes, I'll keep that in mind."

Penny feels just the right amount of nervous excitement, mixed with a pleasant rush of motivation.

"I'll see you on Monday, then. Oh, I almost forgot,
take this with you. It's the train schedule." Dallergut
holds out a fine-print timetable. "The train schedule is
listed by minute. Take the one at the stop closest to your
house around seven o'clock. I'll take one near the store."

"Okay, see you on Monday!"

As soon as Penny steps out of Dallergut's office, she
manages to find information about the train stop closest
to her house amidst the tiny printed text on the train
schedule. She circles it with a red ballpoint pen.

Grocery store "Adria's Kitchen" Stop–Departs at 6:55 a.m.

At the bottom of the timetable is a note of caution in bold letters.

*** Commuter trains are not private vehicles.
Please be punctual.**

Penny stares at her pass and the train schedule for a long time. She grins shyly, her fingertips tracing over the name *Penny* on the pass. Her world has suddenly expanded, and the anticipation of exploring the district mixes with a newfound sense of complete belonging, enveloping her in such delight that she feels full.

Penny carefully tucks her belongings into her handbag and leaves the store, moving along the now darkened streets of the shopping district with a more buoyant stride than usual.

TWO

THE CIVIL COMPLAINT CENTER

Monday morning is usually more tiring than any other morning. It doesn't help that today, the weather is dreary and damp.

Penny arrives at the commuter train stop closest to her house on time, though this comes at the expense of the breakfast she skipped. She checks the employee badge hanging around her neck, then slips her hand back into her coat pocket. She went to sleep late last night and finds herself yawning so hard that her jaw starts to feel stiff.

The train stop is right in front of Adria's Kitchen, a grocery store on a hill near Penny's house. It has been open since early morning and Penny observes that it is packed with eager shoppers eyeing the morning sales.

Penny stands politely out of the way of customers going in and out of the store. Half a dozen commuters have already gathered at the train stop, each lost in their world, wearing earphones and crossing their arms—a clear sign of *No small talk invited*. They all look like they want to spend some quality time alone before delving into the workday's demands.

Penny's excitement mounts as she prepares to board the commuter train. But despite her excitement, she isn't looking forward to her final destination: the Civil Complaint Center. The name itself exudes an air of sternness and formality, as administrative offices usually do, which instinctively makes her tense up a little.

It's a place you want to avoid if you can help it . . . It's an uncomfortable place. Penny remembers Mogberry's remarks, part advice and part warning.

Within minutes, the crowd grows around the stop. Several commuters chatter behind Penny, sipping hot drinks that smell of rich grain.

"I hear the new Director of the complaint center brought in all her connections as soon as she took office."

"That's what you do when you take over. You want to clear out your predecessor's shadow and start with a clean slate. That's also when you're most motivated. Ouch! That's hot!" a man with a gravelly voice says, as he chokes on his beverage.

"I bet the Dallergut Dream Department Store is going to be pretty busy."

Penny's ears perk up.

"I suppose so. The more customers you have, the more complaints you'll get."

"Never mind them, we have our own affairs to worry about. If we can't get the department store to buy our new product line again, we're in trouble. I don't want to start a Monday with the boss nagging at me. Oh dear, and now it's raining."

Raindrops begin to fall on Penny's head. People gather under the grocery store's awning, but Penny's lucky enough to find a spot next to an advertising sign, sheltering her from both the rain and the wind.

**Madam Sage's Mom's Homemade Ketchup
and Dad's Homemade Mayonnaise—**

Newly Updated 2021 Version Now Available
with Deeper Flavors and Emotions
(Contains 0.1 percent Longing)
No Need to Be a Good Cook!
All You Have to Do Is Appeal to Emotions!
Recreate Homemade Flavors
of Your Dear Parents!

The signage shows children joyfully tearing up as they munch on tasty-looking omelets. Behind them, their mom and dad are holding up the advertised condiment bottles, giving a thumbs-up. The omelets are covered with red ketchup, the yellow egg barely even visible.

Penny is staring at the family's goofy smiles, amused,

when a guy in front of her accidentally steps on her feet. He moves past her without an apology, donning earphones and rhythmically bobbing his head to the music playing in his world. Penny takes big sideways steps to avoid him and collides with an incredibly soft and fluffy creature in what feels like a gentle embrace.

"Penny! What're you doing here at this hour?"

The soft creature turns out to be Assam the Noctiluca. He is clutching a hefty shopping bag with both his front paws, and as if that weren't enough, another bag dangles from his tail.

"Hey, Assam. Grocery shopping this early? I'm here to catch the train to work. I finally got my own pass! It's been a year since I started working at the dream department store."

"Wow, already? How time flies! I've also got some good news. I'm going to start taking the commuter train often as well. After getting more career experience and meeting the requirements, I'm finally switching jobs."

"You're switching jobs? Where are you going to work?"

"The Laundry! You know, the Noctiluca Laundry, at the bottom of the Dizzying Downhill. It's every Noctiluca's dream to work there! I've spent thirty years roaming the streets and putting sleeping gowns on people. I've had more than enough experience, but it took me forever to meet one of their important requirements . . ."

"What was the requirement?"

"Well, do you see this blue fur here?"

Assam pulls out his tail, a grocery bag hanging from its end, and holds it in front of his body. When Noctilucas start to fully age, their fur turns blue. But no matter how hard Penny looks at it, Assam's tail isn't blue, but rather a dark ashy color, darker than the rain clouds above them.

"Where?"

"Look here. The fur is turning blue from the inside."

Assam digs up inside his rich tail and shows a pea-sized patch of blue. He looks as proud of this sign of aging as if it were a medal of honor.

"When did you get so old, Assam?" Penny says wistfully as she pats his tail. A long spike of leek sticks out from Assam's grocery bag and pokes Penny in her side.

"Excuse me, Penny, I may be old, but I'll definitely outlive you."

"What?" Penny asks, pushing away the leek with her hand.

"You can't measure a Noctiluca's lifespan in the same way you would a human's. I've been looking forward to getting older because that means I get to work at the laundry. Anyway, I have to go. I need to get home and have breakfast before I go to work. Oh, Penny, looks like the train is coming. The ground is shaking in the distance. I can feel it in my feet."

Assam, using his fluffy front paws, fixes the grocery bag's position hanging from his tail and buoyantly walks away, wagging it from side to side. *No wonder he looks forward to working at the laundry*, Penny thinks. Even if Noctilucas live longer than humans, the daily hustle of dashing through alleys with mountains of pajamas and sleeping socks sounds exhausting to Penny.

Just as Assam had predicted, a train starts pulling into the station from a distance. People begin to line up on the platform. Penny pulls her collar tight and puts her hand over her head to ward off the raindrops as she blends into the single-file line.

The commuter train screeches to a stop right in front of Adria's Kitchen. The train is roofless, like a roller-coaster. Each row consists of two seats, starting behind the driver's seat. The driver pulls a lever, and the waist-high door swings open.

"This commuter train will depart Adria's Kitchen stop at 6:55 a.m. It will make standard stops before reaching the Company District as our final destination," the driver, who looks about Penny's age, calls out to the passengers. "If you prefer a nonstop journey to Company District Central Square, please take the express train, which arrives in eight minutes." Her clear voice effortlessly pierces through the rainy air as if she's had special vocal training. People at the front of the line show her their passes and sit in their desired seats. She checks the pass hung around Penny's neck and nods. A few seats on the train are much larger than the others, with covers on the backrests that read *For Noctilucas Only*. Penny hesitates for a moment, then sits down at the front, directly behind the driver.

"Yuck, it's damp."

Raindrops have pooled on the seats, and the wetness soaks through Penny's coat. There is a retractable overhead covering to keep out the rain, but it hasn't been deployed yet. As other passengers with soaked butts grumble, the driver nonchalantly grabs the bent metal brim next to the driver's seat and, without looking, deftly hooks the end of the covering and pulls it down.

Except for a few people waiting for the express train, most of the commuters take their seats, and once they're sure that no one will be sitting next to them, they seem to relax and enjoy their alone time.

Penny is just about to relax herself when she suddenly feels a hefty presence sit down next to her. The hem of her sky-blue coat is bunched up under the uninvited trainmate's hip.

"Motail! What are you doing here?"

"Hey, Penny! What do you mean? Dallergut asked us to meet him at the Civil Complaint Center. Didn't he tell you that at the salary negotiation?"

"Oh, right, yeah. I forgot that you also got your pass this time."

"Yeah. I left home too early and had some time to kill, so I walked over here from the stop closest to my house. But because of that, I almost missed both trains."

He raises his hips slightly for Penny to pull out her coat from underneath him. As soon as he sits up straight, the train starts moving.

"Motail, what do you think the Civil Complaint Center looks like? It's hard to see it from this distance, so I'm curious."

"I heard that it is famous for its very unique architecture. I'm actually more curious about the testing center above it than the complaint center itself. They have all kinds of materials for dreammaking, and they can even recreate touch and smell sensations. They also test the quality of various dreams there."

It appears Motail knows quite a bit about the place.

"Oh, I wish we could go there, too."

While they are busy chatting, Dallergut boards at the next stop. He's wearing a glossy coat made of water-resistant material and holding a purple umbrella. The driver doesn't even bother to check his credentials, as if Dallergut's face itself were his pass. A man at the back of the train stands up and gives Dallergut a quick bow.

Dallergut walks over to shake the man's hand and says,

"It's been a while, Aber. I hear you've been working for Celine Gluck's production company since last year." He then comes over to where Penny and Motail sit and greets them as he shakes off the water from his purple umbrella. "I see you both made it on time! Good."

Dallergut is about to settle into a seat behind them when the train abruptly jerks to a halt, making his body lurch.

Four Noctilucas are sprinting toward the train, their large bodies flailing. All of them are covered in blue fur, hugging baskets of laundry the size of their bodies.

"Please make sure to be on time," the driver chides them. But she doesn't bother to check their credentials either.

They pull out the laundry from the baskets and pile it on the empty seats. They then stack the empty baskets upside down and hang them over the backrests of the last seat. Their laundry loads are quite hefty. Their work doesn't seem as easy as Assam had made it sound. She begins to worry about whether Assam knows this. An exceptionally blue Noctiluca—perhaps extremely elderly—pounds and flattens out the load, which is on the brink of tumbling off the train.

The train diligently moves along the rails. Penny huddles near the edge of her seat, trying to distance herself from Motail's excited, nonstop chatter and the train's rattling. Her shoulders are damp from the raindrops dripping from the end of the overhead covering.

Far from the center of town, the rails on the horizon suddenly disappear from view. Finally, the Dizzying Downhill that Penny has only ever seen from a faraway distance comes into focus. But it's so steep that she can't even see the bottom.

As they get closer to the drop, Penny's hands start to sweat. She feels like the Noctilucas' laundry is going to fly out. She grows increasingly doubtful of the safety of this rickety old train, which has neither handles nor safety bars.

"Are we . . . going to be okay?" Motail's anxious voice adds to the tension.

Penny sees the driver retrieve a small bottle by her feet. The driver unscrews a rusty stopper next to the steering wheel and pours half of the liquid from the bottle into the stopper's hole. The train lurches and rattles, sharply decelerating just before its descent. The train wheels begin to creep downhill, as if they've caught on something. Penny sees the label on the bottle the driver used: *Rebellious*. She hopes the driver managed to get the amount just right.

The train stops completely at the end of a long descent. They are now in a valley between massive mountains.

"We have arrived at the Noctiluca Laundry stop. The time is 7:13 a.m. If your destination is the Company District, please remain seated. The train will depart soon."

"The laundry? Where?" Penny looks around for signs of a laundromat. Dallergut taps her lightly on the shoulder.

"It's behind you, Penny." He nods to a vast cave alongside the train rail. The Noctilucas take their laundry with them as they walk toward the cave. A wooden sign with crooked writing that reads *The Noctiluca Laundry* hangs precariously over the rocks.

"Motail, do you think they can actually do laundry in a place like that?" asks Penny, incredulously.

"Well, air-drying in the sun is not the only way to dry laundry. I'm sure they have industrial-quality dryers," Motail responds nonchalantly. He's less concerned about laundry than he is fixated on what looks like a hole in the mountains in front of them. The hole is the size of a window. He squints to get a closer look. "I think someone's inside that hole."

After all the Noctilucas disembark with their piles of laundry, the train inches forward for about thirty yards, bringing into view the hole in its entirety.

The hole in the mountain turns out to be a snack stall carved into the rock wall. It's hard to tell whether the hole formed naturally, or if the owner drilled it themselves. Wooden menu boards hang on each side of the opening.

The driver pretends to slack off, giving the passengers time to browse the products.

"We have boiled eggs, newspapers and a variety of delicious snacks," the stall owner calls out to the train's passengers, who begin to place orders in a frenzy.

"Two eggs and a newspaper, please."

The stall owner extends the orders to passengers in a basket on a long pole. The transaction is swift and efficient as the passenger puts their money in the basket.

Motail is looking at the menu and shows interest in a brown bottle. "Look, this drink is called Monday Blues Cure. It must be a new energy drink."

Dallergut quickly pulls out his wallet. "Want to try?" he offers.

"May I?"

"Of course. Sir, I'd like to have two bottles of Monday Blues Cure for these two, and one newspaper for me, please."

Others also buy copies of the newspaper, and Penny notices that they all flip to the back page, take a quick glance, and then close it immediately. Dallergut too looks at the back of the newspaper before putting it down.

"Dallergut, can I take a look?"

Penny takes it and flips to the back page, which reveals a slip of paper showing the weekly menus for all the cafeterias in the Company District.

"They must all be buying newspapers just to check the lunch menu. What a clever sales tactic," Penny says as she hands the newspaper to Motail.

"I'd say it's not just clever, it's cunning. Look at this— the actual issue is outdated. They know that people will only look at the back, so they're recycling leftover newspapers." Motail frowns, then folds the newspaper, hands it back to Dallergut and takes a big gulp of his bottle of Monday Blues Cure. The thick liquid inside the dark bottle looks like any ordinary nutritional tonic.

"There's a message on the lid." Motail reads out loud. *"Imagine as you drink: once you get through today, your three-day vacation starts tomorrow."* He immediately chugs the entire bottle.

Penny checks the lid of her bottle. It says *Imagine as you drink: your supervising director is taking the day off today.* The ingredients chart on the side of the bottle lists paltry amounts of emotions: *0.01 percent Liberation* and *0.005 percent Relief.* She presumes the lids must all have different messages, but that all the bottles contain the same ingredients.

Penny decides to give it the benefit of the doubt and takes one big swig. It isn't easy to imagine the absence of a supervising director when there isn't one in the first place. For a moment, something akin to a sense of liberation flickers like a fog, which quickly dissipates.

"Even if this works, it's probably just a placebo effect," Penny says.

"There's no real cure for the Monday blues," Motail replies solemnly, like an enlightened monk.

***

The train starts to move again. Ahead lies a steep climb to the Company District. The rails, built along the sloping rock, look like a slanted ladder on a bunk bed.

The commuter train struggles with the steep incline until it finally succumbs, grinding to a halt and unable to push forward any farther. The driver pops open the rusty stopper by the steering wheel and pours in the contents of another small bottle. She tosses the bottle into a tin can by her feet. The train starts climbing uphill with a roar. Penny suspects the liquid is Confidence.

"Penny, Motail," Dallergut calls. "Look up ahead. We're finally here."

The spectacular view on top of the sheer cliffs and crags slowly reveals itself. The driver pulls back the overhead covering, as the rain has now completely stopped. The sunlight filters through the thick canopy of trees, casting a soft glow on their faces—just the right amount of brightness. The scent of moist soil wafts through the air, tickling their noses.

"Wow, this is so much bigger than I expected. I wonder how many people work there?"

Stretched before them is the Central Square, which is bigger than a soccer field. Many commuter trains traveling to and from the Company District are parked in the depot, with security guards checking the badges of those disembarking.

The entrance of the Company District is marked by two statues, standing reverently as if taking an oath. A brief pledge is carved with solemn calligraphy on the stone pavement of the train's path leading to the depot.

WE HEREBY PLEDGE TO HONOR AND PROTECT THE SLEEP HOURS OF ALL LIVING BEINGS ENTRUSTED TO US WITH UTMOST CARE AND RESPECT.

Upon arrival at the depot, the train comes to a slow stop and the driver makes an announcement.

"We have arrived at the Company District, the heart of the dream industry. If you need to visit the Civil Complaint Center, the Test Center or the restaurant zone, please get off here and proceed on foot. For those commuting to the production studios, please transfer to the respective trains located outside. Please make sure to take all your belongings with you."

One by one, the passengers gather their possessions

and disembark, including Penny, Motail and Dallergut. The moment they step off the train and into the Central Square, Penny and Motail find themselves captivated by the panoramic view that envelops them.

Each structure in the square boasts a distinctive facade. The district is completely different from the Dallergut Dream Department Store, which leans toward classic aesthetics and emphasizes restrained beauty and harmony with its surroundings. Here, each building shows off its character.

As Penny makes her way toward the center, she is drawn to a series of low buildings that look like restaurants. Yet it's impossible to ignore the immediate presence of a massive and distinctive structure at the heart of the Central Square.

"Look, there it is," Dallergut says, pointing to the structure as he walks ahead.

"You mean the one that looks like the base of a tree? That's the Civil Complaint Center?"

"Yes."

Based on its exterior alone, nobody would have guessed its true purpose. It certainly challenges Penny's assumptions about public offices.

The Civil Complaint Center looks like the world's largest tree had been chopped down with an ax, leaving only the trunk. If it weren't for the constant flow of people in and out of the entrance, there would be no indication whatsoever that this structure is, indeed, a building. On top of the structure are multiple colorful house-sized containers, all stacked on top of each other, creating an eccentric sight. It looks as if the containers had been blown away by a typhoon and landed haphazardly on a tree stump.

"Dallergut, are those containers above it also part of the office?" Penny asks, scurrying to catch up with him.

"That's the Test Center—a facility where the dreammakers prescreen and test their dreams before they release them to the public. They also troubleshoot issues postrelease. Sellers like us can meet with the dreammakers at the Test Center. It shares its entrance with the Civil Complaint Center, but once you're inside, the Test Center is completely separate. There's an elevator that takes you there. It's pretty cool once you're in."

Penny makes an eager face, one that shows her desire to get a peek inside, but Dallergut cuts her off. "For today, we're only stopping by the Civil Complaint Center. By the way, where's Motail?" Dallergut looks around.

Motail has veered away from the Civil Complaint Center, and is moving toward a group of people who appear to be waiting for their trains to the dream production studios.

The signs read *Celine Gluck Films*, *Studio Chuck Dale*,

Keith Gruer's Introduction to Dating, etc. The rails stretch beyond the Central Square to a row of colorful buildings.

"Those buildings on the outskirts are dream production studios, right? They look unlike anything I've ever seen," says Penny, wide-eyed. Even from a distance, each building appears to have a different architectural style and is made from different materials.

"That's right. I heard that their preferences were so distinct that they couldn't reach a consensus on a unified architectural design. But isn't it nice to see such unpredictability and diversity?"

Each studio is so distinctive in its style that it's like multiple movies are playing at once, each vying for attention. And to think that each building is a studio dedicated to creating colorful dreams . . . It dawns on Penny, once again, what an amazing place this truly is.

"Whoa, look at that building! It says *Studio Chuck Dale* in big letters. That must be where Dale makes his sensual dreams!" Motail exclaims.

Penny looks to see where Motail is pointing. It's yet another building which appears to be like no other, a pure work of art. It boasts elegant and bold curves, featuring pale red tones on the lower floors while allowing sunlight to permeate the middle and upper floors. Penny thinks the whole building looks like a wineglass with one last sip of red wine remaining.

"Dallergut, what's that studio next to it?" Penny asks, curiously. "The edge of that building looks like it's been crushed."

"That's Celine Gluck Films. You do know who Celine Gluck is?"

"Yes, of course. She creates fantasy and blockbuster movie dreams for the third floor of our store," Penny responds.

"Aha, so that's where she works," Motail says, intrigued. "The discount section on the fifth floor is overflowing with her Apocalypse Series," he adds. "Frankly, I think apocalyptic dreams are a dying trend."

Celine Gluck's production company is a ten-story building with one section of the top floor blown off as if it has been bombed. The spray-paint blobs adorning its walls remind Penny of paintball splatters, and hint at the tension of working in such a high-octane environment.

At the tail end of the waiting line for Celine Gluck's production company stand two weary-looking people. The one on the left has an armful of dream footage material and a stack of papers.

"I binged all these shows and movies nonstop for a week to prep for the new project meeting," they're saying.

"Have you tried watching them at six-times speed? Once you get used to it, you'd be surprised how well you can make out the dialogue," says the other employee.

"Thanks. I'll try that next time. If I pitch another zombie dream to Gluck, she'll explode. I mean, all I can think of is zombies. Are there any original apocalypse ideas?"

"I know what you mean. I can't think of anything else other than an alien invasion. I've changed it up a bit this time, but I'm not sure it'll pass. Avery from the neighboring department is working on a dream where the entire world is covered in salt deserts, and every living being is gradually pickled to death. But I worry the only thing that's going to be pickled to death is her future at the studio."

Celine Gluck Films specializes in cinematic dreams, particularly in the style of disaster movies or superhero movies or movies about alien invasions. Their staff are encouraged to watch soap operas and films for inspiration throughout their working hours. The fact that they get paid to watch films sparks envy among Penny and others. But judging by the tired look on their faces, their job doesn't seem to be as easy as it sounds.

The two employees are about to board a train much smaller than the commuter train. It's mottled with exactly the same colors as the Celine Gluck Films building, making it look like an accompanying set piece. Penny is so immersed in their conversation that she almost follows their train.

"Hey, guys! We don't need to take another train. Come on, let's hurry," says Dallergut, tugging on Penny and Motail's clothes. Penny and Motail hesitantly start toward the Civil Complaint Center with Dallergut, their gazes still fixated on the production studios.

When the three arrive at the Civil Complaint Center, it becomes clear that the wood grain is artificial. The revolving door, constantly turning, mirrors the hue of the tree bark. Dallergut's gang enters through the giant revolving door just as two guests clad in pajamas hop in. They are greeted by a man who looks like someone you'd see at a yoga retreat. He's dressed in a lightweight pale green suit. A tiny grass worm crawls gently over the back of his hand.

"Welcome! The complaint center is this way. Hope you didn't have a hard time finding your way here?" The man kindly greets the two customers in their pajamas first. The gentle tone accompanying his polite gesture had the ability to soothe someone who has been holding in their anger for centuries. Once the customers have been attended to, he finally turns his attention to Dallergut and his party.

"Good afternoon, Mr. Dallergut. I'm Palak from the Civil Complaint Center. I will take you to the Director's office."

Compared to the way he greeted the customers, Palak

is stiff and formal around Dallergut. Penny finds the stark difference in tone slightly annoying, but Motail seems too preoccupied, too absorbed in the surroundings, to have noticed.

The Civil Complaint Center is adorned with potted plants and has soothing classical music playing in the background. Even the ornaments and accent pieces scattered throughout have a comforting green hue. Penny suspects Palak's green outfit may be part of a curated dress code. The temperature, humidity and abundance of green plants all work in harmony to create an incredibly relaxing atmosphere, unlike the rigid image of government offices that Penny had imagined.

"Please come this way. The Director's office is at the end of this section."

"This is like one of those forest yoga getaways. Looks nice. Why were the managers so reluctant to come here?" Motail whispers in Penny's ear.

Palak leads the way, walking toward the central elevator. A large sign is posted at the entrance to a hallway partitioned by a glass door.

LEVEL 1 COMPLAINT CENTER—TROUBLED DREAMS

"Level-one complaints . . . So are there levels two and three, too? Does it get worse and worse?" Motail asks, pointing to the sign.

"That's correct. There are three ways of categorizing complaints, according to their severity. The first is when you have difficulty sleeping, the second is when it affects your daily routine, and the third and most severe is when the very act of dreaming becomes painful. The third is often beyond the capabilities of our staff, so the Director personally sees to such complaints herself," Palak says as he opens the glass door.

The broad corridor curves anticlockwise, appearing to guide people in a circle back to the central elevator. On either side of the hallway are counters like those you'd see in a bank or a government office. What makes this hallway stand out is the arrangement—complainants and counselors sit side by side like close friends rather than face-to-face across the desks. The employees are all dressed in the same green outfit as Palak's.

"Oh, how awful . . . That must have been really hard for you."

Penny hears the soothing voice of a counselor attending to the visibly agitated complainant seated beside her. The customer's vibrant floral pajamas are hard to miss as she voices her grievances.

"And, in my dream last night, I was being strangled by a villain! I was struggling to free myself, and luckily, I woke up just then—and you know what it was? My cat was sleeping on my neck!"

"Ah, it seems to me that this is a case where a dream

is altered based on the customer's circumstances . . ." The counselor puts a hand on her forehead, wearing a grave expression on her face as if this had happened to her. "It probably didn't start as a strangulation dream. It appears to have been a subconscious defense mechanism, altering the dream's narrative to wake you from your sleep. It's quite common. I know it might be challenging, but how about creating a separate sleeping space for you and your cat?"

The next counter, and the next, and the next, are filled with customers complaining about their dreams.

One complainant appears to be so vocal that the complainant next to him looks over, trying to see what's going on.

"It's driving me real crazy, you know! I'll wake up in the morning and walk to the bathroom, take a shower, get dressed, put on my shoes, and leisurely walk out the door, and then I'll wake up and realize it was a dream. So I think, *I'm late, I'm in trouble* and go back to the bathroom to wash up. I turn on the shower, but the water doesn't feel right—it's weird—but I try my best to wash up, and when I do, I realize it's yet another dream. I dreamed about getting ready nearly ten times in a row . . ."

While the complainant speaks, the counselor takes notes and fidgets through the manual. She seems to be new at her job here, and her panic is palpable.

"Just being here makes me feel guilty," Motail mumbles sullenly, slumping his shoulders.

Meanwhile, Palak walks slowly, with his hands clasped behind his back. Penny keeps her eyes on the ground, fearing she might step on the back of his shoes. Dallergut follows from behind, neither urging them on nor speaking.

After passing dozens of counters, they come to a glass door that leads to the second-level reception area.

LEVEL 2 COMPLAINT CENTER—WILD DREAMS

The reception area for Level 2 is similar to the one for Level 1, save for several posters for anger-management breathing techniques. Two-liter bottles of Calm Syrup for Business are also neatly arranged by each window. Apparently, it's impossible to have a smooth consultation here without a warm cup of tea sweetened with Calm Syrup.

Perhaps that's the reason why the complainants here seem calmer than those at the Level 1 counters.

"My dreams constantly jump from scene to scene, but the transitions are outrageous. I'll dive out of the window from three stories up or plunge into the ocean to escape from a villain. I once even sprinted barefoot through fire. So when I wake up, I'm already drained and too disorientated to start my day. I'm so tense it aches like I've been beaten all over." A customer wearing a robe with roomy sleeves calmly voices his complaint as he sips his tea.

"I see. This is not your fault. The blame is entirely on the inexperienced dreammakers and the sellers who thoughtlessly promote these dreams. Even in dreams, there's an instinctive aversion to danger or discomfort, and crafting dreams that blatantly defy basic logic and forcefully impose challenging situations . . . Well, it's irresponsible of both the dreammakers and sellers."

The word *irresponsible* rings loud and clear in Penny's ears as she walks by.

Penny plucks up the courage to speak up. "I think that counselor was a little too harsh with the word choice *irresponsible*. I mean, we don't get paid for dreams that don't stir emotions in real life."

Palak stops and looks back at her. "You sound like you think you sellers are doing the customers a favor, when you're really profiting off of them."

His cutting comment catches Penny off guard, but Motail steps in.

"Of course it's not a favor, but it's true that customers have many different dreams to choose from while they sleep—because we sellers and makers offer a huge variety of dreams."

"Are you saying they shouldn't complain, but should be grateful just to have the privilege to buy any dream? It's easy for you to say. You're oblivious to the reality of how many of them are gravely affected by these dreams. It's clear you work in the bubble of your fancy, jolly department store, clueless and carefree," Palak retorts.

Penny finally sees why Palak has been strangely distant. The staff here are sick and tired of the daily barrage of complaints, and their arrows of resentment are pointed at the dreammakers and sellers, who they think are to blame.

"I've never felt so uncomfortable in my life," Motail whispers to Penny, pouting. Penny, too, is unsettled; she has grown used to seeing eager, mostly satisfied customers at the dream department store.

Is this what it would feel like to run a candy store, basking in the adoration of children, only to step into a room full of resentful dentists? Penny suddenly understands why Mogberry doesn't like coming to the complaint center.

They finally navigate their way out of the reception area and to the door of the innermost office—that of the Director. The door is closed, and a man holding an envelope appears to have just emerged from inside. He greets Dallergut as if they're old acquaintances. Penny recognizes his face.

"It's been a while, Grang Bong. You look good," Dallergut greets him and clasps his hands. The man is stocky and has thick eyebrows.

"That's because I eat well, both in my dreams and in real life."

The man is a dreammaker who goes by the name Chef Grang Bong because he sells real food alongside dreams of Eating Delicious Food at his shop. Mogberry, a regular, introduced the shop to Penny, who has only been there once. Grang Bong's eating dreams are much more expensive than the real food he sells, but there's nothing like his dreams when you're on a diet.

"What could you be doing here? Do people even file complaints against you?" asks Dallergut as he points to the envelope in Grang Bong's hand.

"Of course. Most of them are about how their diet failed after my eating dream because it inspired a craving. Same old, same old." Grang Bong smiles wryly.

Grang Bong takes off, but the others still have to wait.

"Please hold on for a moment until the previous appointment finishes. Now, if you'd excuse me . . ." Palak rushes off to greet other visitors.

Shortly after, the door to the Director's office opens to reveal a group of fluttering Leprechauns, the creators of flying dreams. The complaints against them appear to be printed on small sheets of paper. Each of them is holding a sheet, reading them as they fly in place. They're complaining themselves, flying about so carelessly that they almost bump into Dallergut. Startled, they all do a quick somersault before flying away.

The Director's office smells of an aromatic oil and waterlogged wood. At first glance, it looks three times the size of Dallergut's office.

"Welcome. I'm Olive, the Director of the Civil Complaint Center." She's clad in a meticulously pressed dark green uniform, with sharp, precise angles. She rises from her chair and greets Dallergut with a handshake. Her nails are painted the color of unripe olives, matching her name.

"Hello, I'm Dallergut, the owner of the Dallergut Dream Department Store. These are my employees. They have been with me for a year now."

"It's nice to meet you. I'm Motail."

"Hello, I'm Penny. Congratulations on your promotion."

"Oh, thank you. Please have a seat, everyone. How was your first trip on the commuter train?" Olive asks with a warm smile.

"It was nice, although a little scary coming down the hill," says Penny as she scans Olive's desk. A framed biographical sketch catches Penny's attention, concluding with the notable line *Veteran of thirty years in the Level 2 Complaint Center.*

"If there are complaints against other stores in our neighborhood, I can relay them," Dallergut chimes in. "I know the shop owners are busy, and it can be a hassle to come all the way here."

"Oh, will you? That's kind of you." Olive's expression and tone are reminiscent of a seasoned teacher comforting a fussy child.

"Now, let's see the complaints that have come through for our store, shall we? More than a handful, I presume. I'm getting a little nervous," Dallergut says.

"It's not that many. Anything on the lighter end, such as questions like *What on earth was I dreaming?* have already been handled by our counselors. I've sorted them by floor in case you'd like to review. Here, take a look."

Olive hands Dallergut an envelope labeled *The Dallergut Dream Department Store*.

Dallergut opens it and examines the contents. "These are for Mogberry on the third floor, and these are for Speedo. Nothing for the second floor this time. We've got a few for the fifth floor, mostly about quality issues."

"But our floor's dreams are cheap." Motail shrugs. "You can't expect perfection from an eighty percent discount. Plus, I don't force customers to buy discounted dreams. There's just no way I can stop their instinct for a bargain."

Olive shoots Motail a disapproving glance.

"Okay, now on to the serious ones . . . There are two." Dallergut pulls out two pieces of paper.

Penny can see a snippet that reads *Complainant: Regular No. 1 Customer*. Her eyes twinkle with intrigue.

"I'll take care of this myself," says Dallergut as he folds the paper and tucks it deep into his coat pocket. "And this one . . . Hmm, this is going to be tricky, too." He's about to tuck the second complaint into his coat, but changes his mind and hands it to Penny. "Penny, how about you take this complaint? This came for the first floor, which means the front desk. As you know, I've got a lot on my plate already."

"Like the secret event you mentioned at the salary negotiation?"

"Precisely. I could use some of your help on this issue while I work on the event."

"Sure, but . . . You're asking me and not Weather?"

"Didn't you say one of your goals for this year is to bring back our regulars? Well, this could be a start."

COMPLAINT LEVEL 3: WHEN DREAMING ITSELF BECOMES TOO PAINFUL

Attention: The Dallergut Dream Department Store
Complainant: Regular Customer No. 792
"Why are you taking even my dreams away from me?"

* This report is based on the half-asleep complainant's incoherent account, edited for clarity by the overseeing counselor.

"It is rather short," Dallergut says to Olive as Penny is still processing the complaint.

"Yes, as with all other level-three complaints. Had I been the director when this complaint was filed, I would have ensured it was more detailed. Apparently, my predecessor liked to keep them short. As I'm sure you know, Dallergut, there's nothing my office can do for this complainant."

"Well, I suppose there isn't," Dallergut agrees.

"Did somebody try to steal the complainant's dream?" Motail chimes in. He's been looking at the complaint with Penny and can't help but be curious.

"No. No one."

It's strange. Level 3 means the customer was having a dream too painful to dream, but the complaint is "Why are you taking even my dreams away from me?" It doesn't make any sense. Penny is stumped by this enigmatic complaint.

Afterward, Penny and Motail are alone on the train back to their shopping village. Dallergut had asked them to head back ahead of him, as he had other business in the Company District.

Penny stares at her Level 3 complaint, then heaves a deep sigh. "I don't know why this customer refuses to dream now. Do we even have a solution for this?" she asks Motail.

"No idea. Let's tackle it one step at a time. You know, buying dreams is like buying any other good. Like buying food or a video game."

"Right."

"Penny, maybe what the customer means by having their dreams taken away is that there is no dream they want to buy. Think about when you go shopping. When do you walk into a store and end up leaving empty-handed?"

"When I don't find what I'm looking for. But there are tons of dreams at our department store alone."

"Yeah, that's true. I don't think it's about the lack of variety. It's like food. Maybe similar to how there are so many delicious kinds of food, but options are limited when it comes to healthy or vegan food?" Motail reasons.

On the rattling train, they try to think as hard as they can, but nothing comes to mind.

Penny gasps quietly.

"I think we should meet Customer No. 792 in person."

THREE

WAWA SLEEPLAND AND THE MAN WHO WRITES A DREAM JOURNAL

The man decided to go to bed early. He switched off the lights, gripped the headboard and nestled into the bedsheets, unfolding his tousled comforter as he lay down. His dog followed him into the bedroom, the tip-tap of its footsteps halting just a short distance from his bed. It plopped down on its cushion, settling into a comfortable position and taking a deep breath. And with that familiar sound, all the tension in the man's body dissipated.

Everything is safe here in my room.

Each night, the man looked forward to his favorite activity: dreaming. Tonight was no exception as he closed his eyes and pictured in his mind a particular dream he longed to have. Though he hadn't been dreaming as much lately, he was still hopeful that tonight would be his lucky night.

He closed his eyes and slipped into a light slumber.
The sound of people murmuring echoed in his ears. In
the midst of his shallow sleep, a shred of his remaining
consciousness soon acknowledged the disappointing realization that tonight would be another dreamless night.

In his sleep, he stopped briefly at a bustling store,
sensing the ebb and flow of people before deciding to
change course and head in the opposite direction. An
employee spotted him and tried to call out to him, but
her voice was lost in the crowd.

The man continued to sink deeper into sleep.

But he didn't dream that night.

When Penny spots Customer No. 792 standing outside the store, she runs out and shouts to him. But the
customer seems oblivious and, in the blink of an eye,
disappears into the crowd. Usually, Penny doesn't solicit
customers, but today, she cannot afford to let him slip
away. It's been a week since she saw his complaint, and
this is the third time she's witnessed him approach the
entrance, only to leave again.

Penny thinks about his complaint. *Why are you taking
even my dreams away from me?* She'd imagined someone
tackling him and snatching his dream away every time
he came by the store. But instead, he keeps standing

outside the store each night without actually entering. Penny can't wrap her mind around why.

She finds herself distracted. She keeps an eye on No. 792's Eyelid Scale, checking to see if it points to REM sleep. It's become her habit to step outside the store and sneak a peek whenever she senses footsteps approaching, hoping it might be him.

★ ★ ★

After failing to bring in No. 792 yet again, Penny returns to the shelves on the first floor to resume her work. In her haste to catch No. 792, she'd left boxes haphazardly strewn about, causing other customers to trip and stumble.

"I'm so sorry. Let me clear these up for you right away."

It's quiet enough at the front desk for Weather to handle things alone today, so Penny has been assigned to organizing the shelves. Her hands are occupied with cleaning up the mess, but her mind remains plagued with thoughts about No. 792.

Why does he leave without coming in? Penny continues to wonder. Is it really because there are no dreams that he wants at the store, as Motail said? But the products are flying off the shelves, and customers are clearly loving what's being offered. So the product list is probably not the problem. Is it that No. 792's taste has suddenly changed?

Penny has too much work today to be this preoccupied with No. 792. The first thing she has to do is fill the empty shelves.

On the first floor, behind treasured dreams, award-winning products are selling like hotcakes. Winners from the Year-End Awards get featured with one-line reviews and recommendations from different dream critics, further whetting the customers' appetites.

Dreams boasting impressive tags like *Grand Prix Winner* and *Nominated for Best Dream for Three Consecutive Years* tend to sell best. Other tags, such as *Recommended by Award Winners* or *Critically Acclaimed* also grab customers' attention. Ideally, every customer would try out the full range of dream products, but it makes sense that they rely on critics' recommendations and catchy titles instead.

"Weather, I think we should make a separate display area for Wawa Sleepland's 'Living Rainforest.' It's getting more and more traction," says Penny.

"It's okay, just leave it," replies Weather, as she secures a stray red curl with a bobby pin. "Production can't keep up with the sales anyway, and the shelves will be empty before long."

However, even among the dreams that are popular with critics, there are exceptions. Yasnoozz Otra's "Living as a Bully of Mine for a Month" is one of them. It is a masterpiece that was nominated for the Grand Prix last year, but its sales were extremely low. Penny finds it rather surprising, considering Otra's reputation as one of the Legendary Big Five.

Penny moves Otra's dream products to the front of the display stand so they can get more visibility. After brushing off her work apron, which has picked up some dust from the products, she returns to the front desk.

"Great work, Penny," Weather compliments her.

"It's a breeze now," Penny says cheerfully, but inside, she's still troubled about No. 792.

* * *

Weather diligently lubricates the Eyelid Scales whenever she detects any stiffness in their movement. Her meticulous attention to detail pairs perfectly with her full-time responsibilities at the front desk, a role that befits her position as a manager. When she applies an oil infused with dried grass to the rigid pendulums resembling eyelids, they start to move up and down smoothly.

"Penny, can you open the small bottle there for me?" Weather nods her chin toward the oil sitting on the front desk.

Penny retrieves the bottle, uncaps it, and slowly pours its contents into a larger bowl.

"So . . . Got anything for No. 792?" Weather casually prompts as she coats a thin brush with the oil.

"No, nothing. Still no progress. If he comes inside the store, I could strike up conversation, but he just loiters outside and then leaves."

"Ah, I see."

"Why do you think he believes his dreams have been taken away? It's not like there are any pickpockets around here." Penny struggles to make sense of it as she carefully returns each lubricated set of scales to its designated place. "And even if his claims were true, he could have come to us first, yet he went directly to the Civil Complaint Center. Why? I have so many questions."

"Our sleeping customers often process things instinctively and take immediate action compared to when they're awake in real life. Perhaps he intuitively knew the answer wasn't in our store. And . . . To give you a hint, he might already know that the answer lies within himself," says Weather in a serious tone, wrapping a white cloth around the oil-coated brush.

Weather seems to know something about No. 792, yet clearly wants Penny to unravel it on her own—an approach Penny appreciates. But the hint doesn't provide clarity, only more mystery.

"If the answer lies within him, I need to get to know him. But how . . . ? When I see him next time, should

I run up to him and start talking to him? Or would that be too pushy?"

"Perhaps we can start by reviewing our records of him. Fortunately, he's a regular, so we should have his information," says Weather as she tightens the bottle lid.

"The only record we can look up right now is his purchase history, though . . . Oh, wait! Yes! I'm such a fool—why didn't I think of that? I'll look up his recent purchases. Maybe there were issues with the products he bought in the past."

Weather takes off to repair other unstable Eyelid Scales, leaving the front desk to Penny. During the downtime, Penny turns on the Dream Pay Systems, which monitors inventory and reviews. She scans through No. 792's purchase history, occasionally casting a glance toward the front desk in case there are any customers seeking help.

The records show that No. 792 started having frequent dreams a few years ago, which was around the time he was registered as a regular.

A noticeable pattern in the purchase history is his distinct preference for Wawa Sleepland's dreams. The last dream he purchased was "Living Rainforest," last year's Best Art award winner, known for its breathtaking nature scenery.

Wow, he got to dream a lot of Sleepland's work. Penny can't help but feel a tinge of jealousy. All out-of-town customers like him can afford to dream such dreams, as they pay with their emotions, while locals like her have to pay in gordens. For her to buy that many dreams by Sleepland, she would have to starve for months. Dreams by the Legendary Big Five often come with a much higher price tag compared to those of other dream-makers. However, for the Dallergut Dream Department Store, it's not a loss at all: the emotions that No. 792 paid for the dreams are far richer and more colorful than those paid by anyone else purchasing the same dreams.

No. 792 didn't just pay with the usual emotions like Refreshed, Surprised, or Wonder. Oddly, he also paid for the "Living Rainforest" with a small amount of Loss. *Loss?* That doesn't seem like a fitting emotion. Why did he have such mixed feelings?

Penny sifts through the dream reviews, grasping at straws. They are usually one-line reactions, quick and simple thoughts right after the customers have their dreams. Most of them are as trivial as *Why is it already morning? I feel like I just went to sleep a minute ago* or *I think I just had the happiest dream, but I don't remember a thing* or *What did I just dream? Should I buy a lottery ticket or something?* Penny would usually just skim through them.

She clicks on No. 792's review for "Living Rainforest." Surprisingly, the review is long, like a journal entry. Dallergut did mention that dream journals were hard to come by. She was lucky.

January 15th, 2021

I'm recording all the details to capture the feelings and sensations from my dream.

I used to think the sky was blue, and the mountains were green. Turns out, there are more shades to every color.

In the dream, the rainforest's colors kept changing like an organic, living being. It was a captivating scene to behold. The sky was azure blue, and the afternoon leaves flaunted different shades of yellow and green. The dew-kissed blades of grass were so vividly green that I found myself overwhelmed by this medley of unique blue-greens, grateful to somehow still be able to discern each distinct hue.

Was the real world as beautiful as the one I saw in my dream?

But recently, even in my dreams, I find it hard to see. And I'm scared. The fear of going to bed has grown intensely painful. So much of my life has been taken away, but losing my dreams was something I never expected.

I wasn't prepared for this. But I know that even if I had been prepared, it would be too much to bear.

If there really are people who make dreams like in the movies and novels, please let me keep dreaming. I beg of you.

Please don't take my dreams away from me.

Penny stares at the plea at the end of No. 792's dream journal. These words echo his filed complaint.

★ ★ ★

As soon as the man woke up, he reached over to turn
on the light switch. He could sense the room was now
much brighter; his vision could not distinguish objects,
but he could make a very faint distinction between light
and dark. He stretched lightly and gently petted Bandy,
his service dog, who was at the foot of the bed, then he
headed to the kitchen for some water, which he always
stored in the same spot in the refrigerator. The skillful
movement of his hands and the smoothness of the process eased his frustration.

Sipping the cold water, the man retraced his memory
of the previous night. He didn't recall seeing anything in
his dream. And the number of nights where he couldn't
see in his dreams had been increasing lately.

The man had lost most of his sight six years ago due
to a sudden and rapidly progressing illness. Before that,
he hadn't realized that most cases of blindness were ac-
quired. He'd vaguely thought that people were born
blind. Like most people in the seeing world, he took
sight for granted, something too basic and natural to
be considered a capability. Upon the initial diagnosis,
he'd thought the illness would linger for a week or so
and then naturally resolve on its own. When the doctors
explained that he would lose his sight permanently, he'd

had no choice but to come to terms with the harsh reality.

People around him complimented him on his remarkable mental strength. Even he found his own calmness and rationality remarkably strange. Experiencing something so traumatic can sometimes clear your head and help you stay focused on what needs to be done, and that's exactly what happened to him. His share of grief fell to his family instead, who mourned on his behalf.

His only focus, in those early days, had been on his immediate survival. Perhaps his body knew that the biggest threat was his own emotions.

He desperately immersed himself in learning to adapt, determined not to be consumed by despair. First and foremost, he had to learn how to walk again. He practiced navigating obstacles with his cane and became adept at walking alongside walls. With the support of his family and many helping hands around him, he learned to walk around his home on his own in a surprisingly short amount of time.

Was it because he expended every last bit of his remaining senses? Strangely, ever since his rehabilitation training, he'd been aware of his surroundings in a way that was entirely different from before. His world felt both clearer and denser. The number of steps he took onto the sidewalk in front of his house, the uneven pavement and broken tiles, the different smells that wafted in from a nearby restaurant at different times of the day . . . He marveled at how much information he had overlooked before.

Reclaiming his lost routine, piece by piece, was as gradual as stamping and stuttering through learning braille, but it was a tangible accomplishment, one that brightened his life one day at a time. It suited him much better than lying still in his room.

The man was slowly pushing the boundaries of what he could do on his own. One day, without family or peer buddies to help him through school, he entered the campus convenience store—a route he had practiced countless times. As he stepped into the small store, the rhythmic beeping sound of barcodes being scanned at the till greeted him. Adjusting his gait and tapping noisily with his cane, he found he could sense the anxiety of those around him through the sound of their movements. They seemed unsure what to do around him. They courteously pressed themselves against the wall, making way for him in the narrow aisle. Grateful and apologetic, all he could do was walk forward.

The man headed straight to a beverage refrigerator and opened its door. He felt for the top of a soda can and read the braille—it said *beverage*. There was no other information about its brand or kind: most canned drinks just say *beverage* in braille. But he'd come prepared for that scenario. Remembering the location of his favorite drinks, he grabbed the one in the middle fridge, on the far left, just above his chest. *Is this the right one?* he could have asked the staff, who would have been happy to tell him.

But that day, he needed the small success of making a purchase on his own. Plus, he didn't want to bother the clerk, who was tirelessly serving customers at the till alone, scanning barcodes one after another. Frankly, he wanted to pretend nothing had changed, that he was the same as he'd been when he'd had normal eyesight.

He used to be the kind of guy who went out of his way to help others. He would often be commended for his perceptiveness and good manners. He didn't want to lose the person he had been before he lost his sight.

But perhaps his yearning played too big a role. When he popped the can and took a sip outside the convenience store, he realized it wasn't his usual drink, and his willpower, which had served him well till now, crumbled. He hadn't anticipated that the sodas might be rearranged. In reality, this incident was so trivial. He could have simply shrugged and said *I'll make sure to ask next time*. In the grand scheme of things, it was nothing.

But that day, the realization that he might never be the same again, that he had lost not only his sight but also himself, consumed him. The words of his neighbors, whom he had always thought of as kind and gentle, began to replay in his head, one by one: *How pitiful, a young man having to go through this!* It suddenly pushed his buttons, and he could not take it anymore.

Nobody feels more pitiful than I do for my life. Yet, here I am, standing strong because I've overcome it!

The man tossed his cane aside, collapsing at the base of the empty stairs near the convenience store. He was barely managing to suppress the urge to wail when he felt someone approaching.

"Can I help you?" She picked up the man's cane and placed it within reach.

"Thank you."

"I'm a counselor at the school here. You're welcome to come by sometime. I can leave my number and the office address in a voice memo on your cell phone if that works for you."

The man couldn't respond.

As he attempted to rise, she gave him a discreet helping hand and said, "You looked like you wanted to sob. It's not something anyone could ignore."

On his way back home, as the counselor saw him off, the man reflected on what it would mean to spend the rest of his life relying on and constantly feeling indebted to others.

What kind of person can I be to others? How will they see me? Someone whose achievement is, at best, fitting into society, being self-reliant, and avoiding causing any inconvenience? Someone who works tirelessly not to be a burden to their family? Is this now the best-case scenario for the rest of my life . . . ? He'd never thought that the benchmark for *best* could be downgraded to the extent that it now had.

That day, the man returned home and slept for two whole days.

Sleeping was one of his few joys. It was something anyone could do, just by closing their eyes. It didn't take him long to discover that he could see when he dreamed, and it felt like salvation. What he saw in his dreams was even more beautiful than reality. Knowing he could fall asleep and dream again was the only thing that kept him going through the day.

Over time, he got a service dog named Bandy and began to have regular sessions with the counselor, who helped him shape together a new daily routine.

Then, he started having nights where he couldn't see, even in his dreams. It was painful to accept the reality that he had yet more to lose. He desperately wished for an exception to the theory that dreams are woven from memories, and that the more memories he had of sightless days, the more his dreams with sight would diminish.

It was already past midnight, well past his usual bed-time. Tomorrow, he would have to stop by the coun-selor's office. Bandy, seemingly aware that he had plans for tomorrow, whined and nudged at his feet.

"Why am I still awake? All right, I know. I'll go to sleep. Good night to you too, buddy."

The man fell asleep at the same time as he heard his dog gently drifting off.

✱ ✱ ✱

In tonight's dream, the man is with his service dog. Bandy presses against his leg, a comforting gesture to let him know he's there. But the man can't see tonight, just like in his real life before he fell asleep.

Disappointed, he is about to turn around, much like he did last night—but then a voice calls out to him.

"Wait a minute, Customer 792!"

"Who? Me? Who is this?"

The voice is breathless, possibly from sprinting to reach him. "My name is Penny. I work at the Dallergut Dream Department Store."

"The department store? What brings you here to see me? I'm not in the mood to buy a dream today."

"You don't need to. There are some guests at the dream store who'd love to meet with you. If you can do me a favor by meeting with them? You will surely love them!"

"I don't know whom you're talking about. I cannot see them."

"That's okay. They'd love to chat with you. You've technically met them before. Here, let me guide you. Would you mind holding onto my arm?"

The man's service dog, Bandy, is not on guard. In fact, his tail is happily wagging, gently nudging his owner's knee.

What if they're dangerous?

"This must be your friend. What's the dog's name?"

"Bandy. He is a service dog. His name means *firefly* in Korean."

* * *

The man walks into the department store with ease, either thanks to Penny's superb guidance, or possibly because his feet have already memorized the way in.

He hears a sizable crowd chattering in the corner.

"Did you see Wawa Sleepland? She just went into the staff lounge. She is so much prettier in person."

"What about Kick Slumber? I'd be so nervous around him, I wouldn't utter a word! Such a great couple."

They sound as excited as if they'd just spotted a major celebrity.

"We're about to enter the staff lounge. Two guests are waiting for you inside," says Penny, opening the creaky door to usher the man into a warm space, its coziness palpable against his skin.

The man feels the presence of others in the room. Tensing up, he stands close to Bandy. Once more, Bandy doesn't show any sign of alarm. He just wags his tail as he lies down comfortably by his owner's feet.

"We're here. I'll step out so you all can talk freely. Please make yourself comfortable. Oh, and this is . . ." Penny releases her arm from the man and with a flourish, spritzes something into the room.

The man can feel the small droplets landing on his arm. A scent resembling the smell of leaves reaches the tip of his nose.

"This is a perfume that helps you organize your thoughts. I borrowed it from Mr. Dallergut. Hope it helps." Guiding the man into a single-armed chair, Penny closes the door and leaves.

The two unidentified guests finally speak.

"Hello, Customer 792. I'm Wawa Sleepland. I make dreams with beautiful landscapes."

"Nice to meet you. My name is Kick Slumber. I create dreams where you can become an animal, like a killer whale or an eagle. Sorry for the sudden introduction. It must be confusing to be called into a meeting with strangers."

"Uh, hi. I'm Tae-kyung Park. So you guys create

dreams . . . That's wonderful. But what business do you have with me? And how do you know me?"

"We saw the dream journal you sent us. I'm the creator of the dream 'Living Rainforest.' If you recall, it's about observing the landscape of a rainforest changing with the passage of time and light."

The perfume that Penny spritzed surrounds them with the aroma of fresh leaves and calls to mind a forest scene.

"Ah, I remember! It's my favorite dream. You're right, I wrote a dream journal after I had it—and you read it? Wow . . . Unbelievable . . . I mean, I'm amazed and a little embarrassed."

"You shouldn't be! If you write a dream journal after having a dream, it gets forwarded to the department store. Penny kindly showed me the dream entry you wrote, and I was as delighted as if I had received a precious letter from a fan," says Sleepland.

"I was told you're blind. How long has it been? Have you got used to it?" asks Kick Slumber, getting straight to the point.

"Yes, I'm quite used to it. It's already been six years."

"Six years isn't much time to adjust fully. I was born without the lower part of my right leg. I guess I'm lucky that I didn't have to learn to adapt. It's all I've known."

Kick Slumber has a knack for making uncomfortably personal things feel like no big deal.

The man decides to speak frankly. "You open up and share with me like I'm no stranger. I'll be honest. I find this situation a little awkward."

"I'm speaking openly with you because you'll probably forget your encounter with us when you wake up. It's embarrassing, but we've become so famous around here, and there aren't many people we can confide in. I know it sounds selfish, but I need friends like you, and so does Wawa Sleepland. So here we are. How about you take advantage of our encounter today in the same way?" As Kick Slumber speaks, he adjusts his posture, settling into his creaky chair.

"Perhaps it's a generous gift from God that your world and ours are connected through sleep. We can be dream-friends who can tell each other anything." Wawa Sleepland's convincing voice fills the room.

"Someone you'll forget when you wake up from the dream . . . That's not so bad."

Sensing the man is agreeable, Sleepland and Slumber start to chat as if they haven't spoken for months.

"I was ten when I decided to pursue becoming a dreammaker. One of the first dreams I ever made was running in a vast field. I wanted to be able to run, at least in dreams. It was immature of me to show it off to a classmate of mine when I didn't even have a dreammaking license. I said to him, 'Do you want to see a dream I made? It's pretty good for a first attempt.' And you know what he said?" Kick Slumber recounts casually.

"What did he say?"

"He said exactly this: 'Hey, you've never even walked on two legs. I bet if you try running in dreams, it's going to be all creaky, like having crutches attached to your legs.' A mean little guy, wasn't he? So I said, 'Well, I'm going to make a dream where I dive and fly like an animal, too, and you've never done that either, have you?' He just snorted, like he was daring me to try."

The man is momentarily at a loss, unsure how to react to Kick Slumber's story.

Kick Slumber notices the man's puzzled look and laughs heartily. "You just made a face that was quite the sight. Trying so hard not to feel sorry for me, aren't you?"

"Well, I know I used to hate that look from others myself. So, what happened after that? Did you really create a dream about diving and soaring like an animal?"

"Three years later, I won the Grand Prix at the Dream of the Year Awards for my dream 'Crossing the Pacific Ocean as a Killer Whale.' I was just thirteen years old."

"How did you do that? Where did you find the strength to push forward? I know nothing about creating dreams, but it must have been tough for you."

"All my strength comes from my happiness, and it's the longing for that happiness that drives me. I'm often told that I offer hope for people with disabilities, which is nice, but most of what I do is for my own happiness. You can't spend your whole life being someone else's hope. It goes back to my first dream. It was from the perspective of a killer whale cruising out to sea. That killer whale was me. I just wanted to be free from all the limitations of my world. I didn't want to be defined by a one-legged disability. I wanted to be a killer whale, exploring the vastness without needing two legs—and you know what? That is exactly what happened. I thought I would die if I jumped into the ocean, but there was a bigger world down there. Now, I'm so grateful for my circumstances. Had I been someone with two legs who could run on the shore, I wouldn't have even tried to jump into the ocean." Slumber isn't holding back.

"That's incredible. I still struggle with what other people think of me, even in the small things I do. It's tough for me to focus on myself because I'm always worried about people pitying me or not knowing how to deal with my situation."

"Technically, we can never see ourselves through someone else's eyes. We just make assumptions based on how they react around us. Sometimes, too much information obscures the truth. It's like what they say: nothing is what it seems. And because it's impossible to know what they're seeing, anyway, you might as well imagine the face of someone rooting for you. Which is, in fact, how we're looking at you right now."

"Someone rooting for me . . . You're right, there are so many people who have helped me: my family, my friends, not to mention my counselor, who's been a real pillar for me." The man continues earnestly, "If I didn't have a disability, I'd definitely want to be that person who looks out for others and gives back the same kind of support and understanding I've been lucky enough to receive."

"Actually, you know what? You're already helping others. You might not realize it, but you saved me from my slump," says Wawa Sleepland. "I was just a student who loved art. Even when I started yearning to become a dreammaker, my only goal was to design the kind of sceneries I'd always longed to see on the canvases of dreams. I have a knack for choosing beautiful colors, but I lack the intricate skill set to create dynamic scenes like Kick here. Yet I wanted to understand why I remained in the unstable and painstaking career of dreammaking. After a decade in this business, I'd been feeling quite burned-out. Then, I stumbled upon your dream journal and realized I'm in this line of work for people like you. You have no idea how much that single realization has helped me." Her voice is full of sincerity.

"Perhaps your difficulties are shaping you into a better version of yourself," Kick Slumber blurts out.

"What do you mean?" The man is confused.

"You started to see how much it means to receive someone's help. People can have the same experiences but perceive them differently, and you're the kind of person who wants to help others as much as you've been helped. Now, what do you say? Doesn't it make you reconsider what defines you? You should set aside how you think you're being perceived and take a deep look inside your heart."

"Can I really do that? I fear my disability is growing at such a pace that it's starting to overshadow every other part of me. But . . . But I'm not just a blind person. I'm Tae-kyung Park." Tae-kyung musters up the courage to declare what he has always wanted to say in front of others.

"I know how you feel. I've been there. I didn't want to be called a *one-legged man*. I wanted to confidently say, *I'm Kick Slumber, who just happens to have one leg that's different from the other*." That was the level I wanted to get to, but it's a big leap from one to the other. And I wanted to meet someone who knew that difference. Someone like you." Kick Slumber lets his words linger.

Tae-kyung can tell that Kick Slumber is summoning the courage to share all of this.

"You see, Tae-kyung, as long as there are dreammakers like us and dreamers like you, no one can take your sleep and dreams away from you. It's up to us makers to determine what dreams we can offer you. All you have to do is close your eyes and relax before you go to sleep," Wawa Sleepland says with confidence.

★ ★ ★

They emerge from the staff lounge, and Penny, who seems to have been waiting, kindly offers Tae-kyung and Bandy her help.

"May I show you around each floor if you have the time?"

"A floor-by-floor tour?"

"It was your daily routine to visit the store before. I suggest it's time to get back to your everyday life."

"You'd help me do that? With a tour just for me . . . ?"

"Of course. I'm just doing my job of providing every customer with the service they need."

They ride the elevator to the fifth floor, where the staff are announcing bargains and customers are frantically trying to snag a decent dream from the pile.

"I don't think there're good ones left for me here." Tae-kyung shrugs as he picks up on the vibe of the crowd.

"Don't worry. Motail will help you. Right, Motail?"

"Absolutely! You see, I don't throw offers like this to just anyone." His voice, Tae-kyung notes, is bubbly. "The next time you swing by our discount section on the fifth floor, I'll have a special dream tucked away just for you."

Bandy barks loudly at Motail.

"Hey, why're you barking at me? I'm not fishy! Don't let your dog's bark fool you, sir. You can trust me. Come visit the fifth floor whenever you can!"

Penny leads Tae-kyung and Bandy away, leaving Motail behind.

"I'm sure Bandy will love the fourth floor," she says.

Tae-kyung and Bandy join Penny in the elevator. Upon reaching the fourth floor, Bandy makes a grunting noise, eager to discover what is inside.

"Check it out, Bandy! Plenty of fun dreams for you here," says Penny. "Go ahead, pick one. Your owner is in good hands with me."

Bandy pauses and whimpers in response.

"I'm okay, Bandy. You can go," Tae-kyung reassures him.

As soon as he gets the permission, Bandy darts toward the low shelves, excitedly hopping from one to another.

"Bandy, no running!"

"No worries, sir. This is a safe place. He doesn't need to be on his best behavior like in other stores. I have a good friend to introduce him to, someone just as energetic and lively as he is."

"Hey, you! Stop right there!"

Somewhere in the distance, Tae-kyung hears the sound of roller skates scraping against the ground, and a man's high-pitched voice comes from the direction in which Bandy dashed off.

"That's Mr. Speedo, the fourth-floor manager, hot on his heels. He looks excited," Penny says.

As they make their way down from the fourth floor to the third, a sense of déjà vu hits Tae-kyung as he realizes the department store feels oddly familiar.

"I remember now. The third floor is where fun activity dreams are, right? I feel like I've been here often."

"You have! It's incredible how the body remembers. I'm glad the tour was helpful. They play the latest pop music all day on the third floor. There are vibrant posters showcasing various products on the walls, and each staff member has their own unique uniform. Let me introduce Mogberry, the manager of the third floor."

Mogberry, who has been waiting for Tae-kyung, greets him. "Good afternoon, sir. We specialize in audiocentric dreams on this floor, and all are excellent options. Be sure to check them out! A study says exposure to various stimuli during sleep can enhance different senses, so in that regard, this dream here is . . ."

The two hurry down to the second floor before Mogberry can delve into an in-depth explanation of all the dreams on the third floor.

The second floor boasts perfectly spaced shelves, making navigation and window-shopping a breeze. Display cases are strategically placed, with only three steps between each. To assist those with visual impairments, each case features a braille sign in a consistent location in every section.

"If you press this button here, it plays a voice guide," says Vigo Myers as he quietly escorts Tae-kyung. "I usually recommend the Memories corner to my customers here on the second floor. It does come with a fair amount of trial and error, but if you're fortunate, you can relive memories from before your eyesight declined. Based on what I've observed, you seem to have a lot of memories, so it's premature to assume that you won't be able to see them again."

Penny thinks that only hearing Myers's voice and not seeing his stoic face would make him seem like the friendliest manager at the store.

"I can tell the dreams on the second floor are your favorite," says Penny.

"You're right. I'm so glad there are memories. Now, I guess that brings us to the first floor?"

"Yes, this is the floor where I work. We sell special and popular dreams." Penny leads Tae-kyung to a new corner on the first floor. "We have also created a section for speciality dreams that were once scattered around. Some come with closed captions for customers with hearing difficulties, and others with sign-language support. I must admit, I only discovered they exist fairly recently."

"It's nice to know there are people making dreams more inclusive for people with all abilities."

"Everyone wants different dreams. That is what I learned during my first year of working here. Some customers dislike foretelling dreams, others enjoy nap dreams—even if they regret it later. And you just need a special dream. That's all. So all you have to do is come inside the store."

★ ★ ★

Tae-kyung was unusually talkative in his sleep that night, prompting Bandy to rise first and gently lick his hand as soon as he woke up. The people from his dream had not yet faded from his memory; their voices lingered in his ears. He tried to recall the details, remembering the warmth of the conversation. But as the voices danced haphazardly around in his mind, fragmenting into words, consonants and vowels, they swiftly disappeared without a trace.

Who were these people in my dream? Neighbors? No, they were definitely strangers.

The people in the dream treated him as if they knew him, but they were clearly strangers—their voices were unfamiliar. But again, that couldn't be right. Maybe it was simply a reimagining of his interactions with nameless people in his life. Although it didn't make sense to dismiss it as random brain activity, he had no choice. There was no plausible way he could have genuinely met someone in his sleep . . .

Tae-kyung sat up in bed and reflected on his dream from the previous night a bit longer. *I think I said something that I should always remember*, he mused. And then the words escaped his lips.

"I'm not just a blind man. I'm Tae-kyung Park."

Unbeknownst to him, the words had lingered in his mouth, echoing throughout the night as he repeated them in his sleep. Bandy observed him and responded with a small bark, as if to acknowledge it. He stood up and gave Bandy a gentle pat.

"Let's make it a good one today," he said, addressing not just Bandy but also himself.

★ ★ ★

After finishing his classes, Tae-kyung walked to the counseling office, his steps harmonizing with Bandy's. Upon their arrival, Ms. Yun, his counselor, graciously held the door open and greeted them.

"Welcome, Tae-kyung. How have you been? Hey there, Bandy."

"I'm great. How are you?"

Bandy quietly took his place and lay down in the office, his leash making a small sound as it hit the floor.

"Bandy seems to be in a very good mood today." The counselor's soothing voice rang pleasantly in Tae-kyung's ears.

"He really likes coming here. He always runs around the big courtyard behind this building after our sessions."

"Bandy, you must be so happy to go everywhere with your brother."

"I really hope he thinks so."

"All right, shall we talk about your dreams again?"

Dreams were their main topic these days. Ms. Yun liked to look into people's minds through their dreams and discuss their significance.

"I had an amazing dream last night. I met quite a lot of people this time. I couldn't see them, but I felt so comfortable around them, as if I'd known them for a long time. Oh, and I think Bandy was there, too. The people seemed so real, like they existed somewhere. The situation, their words and actions were too specific to have been made up by my subconscious. Really strange, isn't it?"

"It's not strange at all. There're quite a few people who have had similar experiences."

"Well, maybe there is another world hidden in our memories," Tae-kyung said excitedly.

"Yes, maybe there really is."

Tae-kyung couldn't see Ms. Yun's face, but he did catch a profound sense of longing in the undertone of her voice.

"Do you remember anything else? I'd like to hear more," she adds.

Tae-kyung senses Ms. Yun's heightened interest. "I wish I could say more, but the more I try to remember it, the faster it slips away. If only I had known, I would have written it down in a journal to preserve my memory. You know how they say records help create memories. Do you also dream often, Ms. Yun? I'd like to hear about your dreams."

"I do dream a lot."

"Have you ever kept a dream journal?"

"Yes. Thanks to that, there are dreams I can still re-member vividly, even if they're very old. Once, I had a wonderful dream where I became a killer whale sailing across the Pacific Ocean."

"When was it?"

"Well . . . It was over twenty years ago. I had it in 1999."

FOUR

A DREAM ONLY YASNOOZZ OTRA CAN MAKE

"Penny, you're here early today." Muth, who's had a night shift at the front desk, greets Penny languidly.

"Good morning, Muth."

Lately, Penny has been getting to work earlier than usual to start her morning routine. First, Muth recounts any unusual occurrences from the previous night, then Penny notes which dreams are running low in stock. Next, she grabs her key packet and heads to the storage room. She sets out dream boxes to go on display in one pile and cuts out an ample supply of wrapping paper and strings for new dreams that will arrive later in the day. Her final task for the morning is to go to the storage room and bring bottles full of dream payments down to the entrance for easy deposit at the bank.

Penny carefully lowers each bottle, one containing a dark red Guilt and the other a silver-gray Regret. Now that her work is done, she pulls out a floor cushion she's hidden in the corner, sits, and takes out her magazine, *Interpretations Better than Dreams*, which she nestles between her waist and apron as she immerses herself in her morning read.

Lately, Penny has grown more curious about life beyond the store. Her recent encounter with No. 792 has heightened her sense of urgency, as she believes she might come across another third-level complaint someday. But studying after work is too tiring, so Penny has started coming to work a bit earlier to focus. Among the substantial reading material available, she has started with the more approachable *Interpretations Better than Dreams*. Some might ask *Who studies with a daily magazine?* For Penny, this daily dose of information from outside the store has proven to be highly valuable.

As well as the backstories of famous dreammakers and industry gossip, the magazine provides a glossary of terms related to the dream industry. It also includes articles on relevant legislation, cost-effective dreams, and dreams with a low probability of failure. Except for the Article of the Month section, which is more specialized, pretty much all the articles are in simple, layman's terms.

Having completed most of her work ahead of schedule, Penny now has the luxury of spending half an hour reading the magazine. She used to do her reading in the staff lounge, but she found it a bit noisy with colleagues eating their packed breakfasts ahead of their morning shifts. She's discovered that she prefers the storage room, where the rhythmic dripping of emotions helps enhance her focus.

Penny slowly flips through the pages of *Interpretations Better than Dreams*, and sits up straight when she spots the name of one of the Legendary Big Five, Yasnoozz Otra.

An Underappreciated Dream

Yasnoozz Otra's "Living as My Parents for a Week," released seven years ago today, is a rare masterpiece. Dreams, by and large, can be categorized into two primary groups based on their genesis. One type draws inspiration from the dreamer's memories, while the other is deliberately woven with the intentions and thoughts of the dreammaker, promising a voyage into the surreal realms of imagination. This ambitious creation by the young Yasnoozz Otra, surprisingly, falls under the former category.

Creating a dream rooted in memory proves to be considerably more challenging. Effectively controlling the dreamer's memories while aligning them with the intentions of the dreammaker poses a substantial headache. Though countless individuals aspire to become dreammakers, this complexity serves as one of the primary barriers to the field.

Yasnoozz Otra took dreams to the next level with a unique twist on this perspective. Her dream is told from the point of view not of the dreamer, but of their parents, who intimately share the same memories as the dreamer. This groundbreaking narrative twist showcases her bold and visionary approach, rightfully earning her praise as a true genius.

Upon its initial release, one critic penned a memorable review recounting his version of Otra's dream, which was entirely from his father's perspective.

At the crack of dawn, the alarm went off in the critic's room. Swiftly, his father rose and silenced the alarm, allowing his son an additional five minutes of undisturbed sleep. Then, with a gentle touch, his father shook him awake. The critic observed it all through the lens of his father's eyes, which looked upon him, the dreamer, with such profound love that he was incredibly moved.

For some dreamers, on the other hand, it's a journey into the memories of weary, exhausted parents. Through their parents' eyes, the dreamers perceive themselves as the living embodiment of their parents' self-inflicted punishment. Confirming the painful truth all throughout the night must be a heart-wrenching experience.

Otra's dreams should be highly regarded for their commercial value, as they are payable in various emotions.

But if I were to guess, the reason Yasnoozz Otra's "Living as My Parents for a Week" didn't secure the Grand Prix of the year upon its release has little to do with talent. I daresay it could be attributed to the reality that there aren't as many good parents in the world as one might assume . . .

Penny is fully engrossed in the article, eager to delve deeper, but duty calls, and it's already time for her to return to the front desk.

"Do you still have 'Living Rainforest' by Wawa Sleepland?" a customer asks as soon as Penny is back at her post.

"Hello. Unfortunately, that dream is sold out. We don't have plans to restock them this week."

Penny is about to recommend Yasnoozz Otra's dreams, which are piled next to an empty shelf, but hesitates. She doesn't want to rush into recommending "Living as a Bully of Mine for a Month" and risk getting the defensive response *Are you implying that I've bullied someone?*

Otra's latest dreams, which the store has paid a hefty sum to acquire, are now gathering dust, rendering the critics' perfect ratings futile. Will they eventually meet the same unfortunate fate of those dreams that go unnoticed, despite their quality, much like "Living as My Parents for a Week"? Although Penny cannot outwardly promote them, she can at least shift the display stand toward the aisle closer to the entrance, hoping they gain more attention.

* * *

"Penny, you're full of energy this morning." Weather arrives at the store with Myers and, noticing Penny wrestling with the display stand, she jumps in to help.

Meanwhile, Myers, dressed as usual in his crisply ironed suit, is heading straight to the second floor—but then he stops dead in his tracks and looks back to the lobby.

Scowling, he points out several vacant shelves on the first floor. "Are you guys going to sit on your hands until all the shelves empty out? There's a whole lot of vacant space here—and there."

Pajama-clad customers cast glances at him.

Penny hurries to the front desk, where she fumbles with the dream boxes stored beneath it, acutely aware of Myers's intense gaze. She swiftly stacks them on the empty shelves. One of them is "Loneliness in a Crowd" by Hawthorne Demona, which won Rookie of the Year and Best Screenplay last year. It depicts a person fading into the backdrop of a bustling city, becoming invisible amid indifferent faces.

"Well, well, what's this? Still pushing last year's winners, with even more critics' blurbs? Anyone can recommend award-winning dreams. You gotta have an eye to spot them beforehand." Myers sneers as he glances at Hawthorne Demona's dream.

Beside "Loneliness in a Crowd," Penny is holding Hawthorne's latest work, "The Naked King." Penny contemplates where to display this, and decides to make room next to "Loneliness in a Crowd." She stacks the boxes there.

Myers stands stiffly, arms crossed, muttering to himself. "What's the deal with 'The Naked King'? The dream's merely about wandering around in the buff, and

customers are shelling out for it with all sorts of emotions, spouting off about it like *Oh my god, I'm strutting
around naked. Is that some subconscious desire to be seen as
I am?* I mean, do they really think I don't see through
their gimmick, an attempt to make a quick buck off
something superficial masquerading as profound?" Myers has been consistently against Hawthorne Demona's
dreams since last year's awards show.

"What a snobbish thought, Myers! Haven't you heard
that dreams are all about interpretation? The customers are free to choose their dreams and interpret them
however they want." Someone is brave enough to give
Myers a scolding.

Penny has to look around to identify where the voice
is coming from. She spots the Leprechaun leader perched
on a shelf, wings folded. He wears a vest that is a tad too
snug for his chubby frame.

"What're you doing here?" Myers tries to lift up the
Leprechaun with his forefinger, but the leader swiftly
flies away.

"I've been out since early this morning, doing some
hard research on best-selling dreams. There's no better place for market research than the Dallergut Dream
Department Store," the Leprechaun says, unapologetic
about his spying. "And believe it or not, your customers
are snapping up Hawthorne Demona's dreams, which

you so hate. They're outselling dreams by the great Yas-noozz Otra," the Leprechaun adds, pointing at Otra's dreams, which are piled high and have clearly failed to gain much traction with customers.

"Sales and cinematic value do not always go hand in hand," Myers says, standing his ground to support Otra.

"But who has the luxury to create dreams that don't sell? Rumor has it that Otra is struggling to finance her dreams, and her newest creation hasn't taken off. Looking at these dream boxes, I'd be worried she might have to sell her fancy mansion soon," the Leprechaun taunts.

"How about you worry about selling your own dreams?" Myers retorts.

"Flying dreams continue to sell consistently well on the third floor," Penny chimes in reflexively without reading the room.

The pompous Leprechaun leader flutters toward the shelves displaying boxes of Kick Slumber's "Flying as an Eagle on the Cliff."

"This dream is but a waste of money," the Leprechaun adds. "If I were the dreammaker, I would have let the dreamer fall from the cliff. Some people believe falling dreams make you taller. Who knows, if you're lucky, you might get Anticipation as a form of payment!"

Myers's tidy goatee and thin upper lip shudder. Penny, sensing the tension, steps back, empty boxes in hand.

Myers's face turns purple and he storms off, his heels clicking as he heads toward the stairs to the second floor.

"Tsk-tsk. Everyone knows Myers got booted from college, and he's still sour that he didn't get to be a dreammaker. It must churn his stomach to see new, up-and-coming dreammakers like Hawthorne Demona," says the Leprechaun.

Myers whips around, glaring sharply at the Leprechaun. Just then, Dallergut opens his office door and steps out into the lobby—just in time, as the Leprechaun may have been about to find himself caught in Myers's grasp.

"I knew those heel clicks were you, Myers," Dallergut squeals with delight. "Will you stop by my office before you head upstairs? I want to revisit the level-three complaint we were talking about the other day . . ."

Penny remembers the two complaints they collected at the Director's office. One had been from Customer No. 792, which Dallergut had assigned to her, and the other had been from Customer No. 1—Penny remembers seeing this scribbled on the corner of the envelope.

Dallergut and Myers disappear into Dallergut's office for a long time.

Penny occasionally checks over the front desk for customers as she begins to sift through the data on the Dream Pay Systems. It takes her less than thirty seconds to find the recent purchase history of Customer No. 1. She immediately recognizes who it is. Customer No. 1 is a woman in her forties who comes in at fairly regular times and buys a variety of dreams from the first to the fifth floor. There is nothing unusual about the purchase list itself, but her recent payments seem odd. Lately, she has been paying with only one emotion, Longing. Whether it was a happy dream, a sad dream, or even an expired dream from the fifth floor, all she's paid with is Longing. As Penny continues to look at the data, she realizes No. 1's purchase history dates back all the way to 1999.

"Weather, when was the Dream Pay Systems implemented?"

"It was 1999, I'm sure. We started using it when we brought in the Eyelid Scales."

Penny sorts the data chronologically in ascending order to see records from 1999. She finds a very interesting purchase history.

Created by: Kick Slumber
Title: Crossing the Pacific Ocean as a Killer Whale
Purchase date: August 20, 1999
Review

It turns out Customer No. 1 dreamed Kick Slumber's Grand Prix–winning debut work in the year of its release, 1999.

Penny clicks on the review right away, excited.

August 20th, 1999

Just woke up from a dream and I feel like I should write everything down before this vivid sensation disappears.

In the dream, I was a gigantic killer whale. I was heading farther and farther from shore, out into the vast sea. The salty water rushing through my nose in painful, gasping breaths, the fear of being caught in waves and not making it out alive . . . these were not my main concerns. I'm most impressed by the overwhelmingly immersive nature of the dream.

Kick Slumber's dream offers freedom, not the precarious kind that leaves you without footing, but the safe kind we all desire. The deeper the sea, the more I felt like I was returning home.

I felt the muscles running from my dorsal fin to my tail. I slammed the tail down hard and lifted it back up, instantly picking up speed. The surface of the water was now the ceiling of my world unfolding from beneath my white belly, my world was now deeper than the sky.

I could see, although I didn't need to. I could already feel the world with my other senses. I leaped to the surface on impulse. The word *impossible* never crossed my mind. My perfect hydrodynamic body breached the surface of the ocean and soared valiantly, cutting through the air.

Suddenly, a tingling sensation swept through my body, one I wasn't sure belonged to me. I started to worry about my previous self that I had left at the shore. I tried to continue swimming, releasing my thoughts into the roaring waves.

"This is where I belong."

As I grew used to the heightened senses, I began to wonder if I had been a killer whale all along. Then, I came to a state where I was neither a killer whale nor a human, where the worlds overlapped and separated from each other. That's when I woke up from the dream.

It feels like an inevitable destiny that I dreamed of the debut work of the thirteen-year-old Kick Slumber at this moment and time. This genius boy may well become the youngest Grand Prix winner this year.

But I guess I will never witness that myself . . .

Anything more than this would be too dangerous . . .

What I've seen and heard so far has been nothing short of amazing. Including the people I've met here.

I wonder what it would have been like had I been born into this world from the beginning.

Dear Vigo Myers, I'm sorry I missed your graduation presentation.

Vigo Myers?

Penny never expected to come across that name in a customer's dream journal. Customer No. 1 knew Myers—knew him well enough to write about him in her dream journal. In 1999, more than twenty years ago.

✳ ✳ ✳

Se-hwa Yun, usually referred to as Ms. Yun, worked as a psychological counselor on a college campus. On her drive back home from work, she was reflecting on a recent session with a student named Tae-kyung Park.

"The people seemed so real, like they existed somewhere. The situation, their words and actions were too specific to be made up by my subconscious. Really strange, isn't it?"

"It's not strange at all. There're quite a few people who have had similar experiences."

"Well, maybe there is another world hidden in our memories," Tae-kyung said excitedly.

"Yes, maybe there really is."

After that conversation, old memories Se-hwa had kept to herself for a long time resurfaced. From the time she was very young until her twenties in 1999, she had been a lucid dreamer. She enjoyed her dreams so much that on holidays when she wasn't at school, she could sleep in her tiny room for hours. Her ability to have lucid dreams was the only special thing about her otherwise normal life.

This ability is a gift from heaven. Maybe I'm chosen.

In the summer of 1999, Se-hwa spent her first college break immersed in dreams. In her dream world, she was an out-of-town customer, but the people of the shopping village were always kind and generous to outsiders.

She could choose where she wanted to go and what dreams she wanted to dream. She enjoyed the journey.

In that realm, she heard a mythical tale that had been passed down through generations—*The Time God and the Three Disciples*. The First Disciple was fixated on the future at the expense of the precious memories. The Second Disciple was unable to let go of the past, and eventually succumbed to deep sorrow. And the Third Disciple bestowed dreams to those asleep.

Se-hwa's favorite place in the dream world was the Dallergut Dream Department Store, established by a descendant of the Third Disciple. Whenever she went there, she would watch the customers come and go, and she would buy strange dreams and try them out one by one.

The tomboyish and curious twenty-year-old Se-hwa spent her nights scouring the discount section on the fifth floor as if on a treasure hunt. She'd also perch for hours in front of the elevator on the fourth floor, observing babies and animals entering to buy dreams. One night, fueled by curiosity, she loitered around the dream-payment storage room to take a peek inside, and had to quickly run away when she was discovered by an unsuspecting employee.

But that didn't stop Se-hwa. Another night, she went to the storage room again, avoiding the eyes of the front-desk staff, and hid in there for hours until she got caught by two members of staff, one of them being Dallergut, the owner himself.

"It's you again! How many times do I have to tell you this place is off-limits to the public? It's for staff only," shouted a female employee with bouncy red curls who looked about thirty years old.

Dallergut, who looked a little older, spoke then. "Weather, I'm sure she heard you. But we should head back. We need to get this Eyelid Scales discussion over with. Any ideas on how to turn the marble wall behind the front desk into a display case? It's going to be a huge undertaking. We'll have to shut down the store for a few days and notify our customers . . ." He looked concerned.

"You're right, we need to hurry." Weather's big eyes seemed to signal to Se-hwa *You should get out of here*.

Deflated, Se-hwa followed them out of the storage room.

"Dallergut, here's the problem. The Eyelid Scales aren't quite complete yet. You've seen how these products in the New Technology Lab fall apart at the last minute. I need someone to test them one last time to be sure. Somebody who can remember all the steps and confirm they're working properly, then communicate all this back to us."

Se-hwa's eyes flashed when she heard the words *Eyelid Scales*. She tailed them into the lobby.

"Excuse me, Miss, do you need something? Why are you following us?"

"I'm just curious about the things you called *Eyelid Scales*."

"My god, you don't know when to stop, do you? Fine. So, what are Eyelid Scales? They're special scales that we designed to keep track of the customers who visit our store. It's made of eyelid-shaped weights that can point to each of their stages of sleep, such as Alert, Sleepy, REM Sleep, etc. . . ."

"Weather, wait," Dallergut interrupted. "You said you needed someone to test the Eyelid Scales and make sure they were working properly. Someone who could remember all the steps and communicate with us . . . That means we'll need an extremely high-level lucid dreamer."

"Yes, that's right—but it's very hard to find one."

"Actually, we have one. We're looking right at her." Dallergut grinned, nodding at Se-hwa.

"How did you know I was a lucid dreamer?"

"You don't seem to hesitate, unlike our other out-of-town customers, and you remember this place well enough to get in and out of the storage room without our guidance, so I figured."

"Well, there goes my secret. Are there any other lucid dreamers like me?"

"There are some, though few visit as often or stay as long as you do."

"It's because this place is full of interesting things I want to know about! It's so much more fascinating than my world. Is it wrong of me to wander between worlds?"

"I wouldn't say it's wrong. Your sleep time is all yours."

"I'm relieved to hear that! It would be such a waste to wake up and forget all about this exciting world. How lucky I am to be a lucid dreamer! I wish I'd been born here, though. If anything, I wish I could leave my mark here."

Weather was happy to have found an excellent tester, but something seemed to weigh heavily on Dallergut as he listened to Se-hwa's words.

"Is everything okay?" Se-hwa asked.

"Why, yes. Maybe we can help you make your mark here. You should be our first customer to be assigned an Eyelid Scale."

"Really? Promise me!"

It seemed as though the test went well. Se-hwa continued to wander around the department store in a daze, waiting for the results of her Eyelid Scale assessment. And that was when she met Vigo Myers.

For a month, Myers had been approaching passersby in front of the department store, looking for an out-of-town customer to collaborate on his college project. "Will you participate in my graduate project?" But everyone just walked right past him.

Until Se-hwa, in a set of ivory pajamas, approached Vigo. "I can be your partner."

"Really?"

The two met frequently at a café, with the graduation project serving as a convenient excuse. With their similar ages and shared interests, they quickly grew close.

Meanwhile, Se-hwa's Eyelid Scale became the first to be displayed on the renovated shelf behind the store's front desk. Engraved with the serial number *0001*, the scales worked perfectly.

Finally, I have made a mark in this world.

The staff began to refer to her as Customer No. 1, and one by one, more Eyelid Scales for other customers were placed on the display shelf. As the days went by, she spent more and more time as a lucid dreamer.

"Vigo, do you happen to know why so many people in my world have dreams that are like puzzles? You know, those strange dreams where they walk around naked or where they become invisible and no one can recognize them? After they have these dreams, they want to decipher the meanings behind them."

"Because those dreams are actually easy to make! Dreams that leave the interpretation up to the dreamer have been around forever. They're just released under different names. I think they're kind of a cheap shot."

"Really? I had no idea. You know what? Maybe by 2020, we can both have the same dream at the same time! You should make it, Vigo."

"That's a brilliant idea! Will 2020 ever come, though? I mean, I still can't believe 2000 is just around the corner. Where will we be in 2020? I hope I will have become a famous dreammaker by then. Winning an award at the Dream of the Year Awards, you know."

The two spent hours talking every day, and Se-hwa kept wearing the same pajamas so that Vigo could easily recognize her.

One day, Vigo invited her to his graduation project presentation.

"Please come to my presentation. I've created a dream I want to share with you. But there will be a lot of people. You should wear a normal outfit when you sleep that night so you won't get caught."

Se-hwa agreed to come, but Vigo's words triggered an unsettling feeling in her heart. She tried to ignore the sinking feeling and went about her usual visit to the department store. Dallergut was working at the front desk alone, carefully cleaning her Eyelid Scale.

"Hello, Mr. Dallergut."

"Hey, welcome back. Wait—is everything okay?" asked Dallergut, catching her conflicted expression.

After a pause, Se-hwa asked, "Putting on regular clothes before bed doesn't make me part of this world, does it?"

Dallergut looked at her wistfully, as if he'd seen this coming. He extended the Eyelid Scale toward her.

"Take a look here. Your eyelids are still closed, aren't they?" said Dallergut. The Eyelid Scale showed they were indeed tightly closed, indicating REM sleep. "They are always closed, every time I see them."

"Yeah . . . Recently, I've been sleeping all day to have lucid dreams."

"But what about your life in the real world?" Dallergut asked gravely.

Se-hwa had been neglecting the reality that, no matter how freely she roamed in her dreams, in her real life, she had shut herself away from the world for the entire summer vacation, lying still in her bed in her small room.

Her mind seemed to go blank at Dallergut's question.

"What am I supposed to do now?" she asked. "Should I go deeper into this world or go back to where I came from before it's too late? I have no idea where I belong anymore. What if I suddenly can't have lucid dreams anymore? Or is that better for me? I don't think I belong anywhere. I'm scared."

"It's okay, dear. You're going to be fine. There's still time to make it right. Could you wait here for a second? I have a dream that might be perfect for you. We only have one in stock, but I'm glad I didn't sell it to someone else."

Dallergut hurried to his office and came back with a dream box for Se-hwa.

"This is a brand-new release. I can guarantee the quality."

The box had dark blue, translucent wrapping paper that looked ocean-deep.

"What kind of dream is this?"

"It's titled 'Crossing the Pacific Ocean as a Killer Whale.' Of all the dreams at our store, I think this one should be a perfect fit for your situation."

That was when Se-hwa had the dream by Kick Slumber. As soon as she woke up, she wrote in her dream journal and came to the Dallergut Dream Department Store again.

Having read her review, Dallergut said, "This world is the shore for you, the shore of your dreams. It may be scary right now, but the farther you go from this shore, the deeper you'll get back into your real world. Looks like you seem to have caught on already while dreaming this."

"Yes. I really needed this dream. It helped me realize what I need to do. That is, I need to stop getting close with the people here . . . Rather than visiting here so often, I should shut my eyes tight, get a good night's sleep, then focus on living life to the fullest in my own world."

"Very well. It's unfortunate, but I think you've made the right decision. There's just one caveat."

"What is it?"

"Your lucid dreaming ability could very well disappear without notice at any time."

"What? Really?"

"Highly advanced lucid dreamers like yourself usually lose the ability before the age of twenty. You've passed that age. So you should be prepared."

"I see . . . That means I won't be able to say a proper goodbye to everyone. Please take care of my Eyelid Scale when I do disappear."

"While you won't be able to have lucid dreams forever, you can always come to visit our dream department store," Dallergut told her.

"But I will no longer remember any of this . . . To me, this is farewell for good."

"We'll always be here. Don't be so heartbroken."

★ ★ ★

Not long after that, Se-hwa stopped having lucid dreams, just as Dallergut had predicted. At first, she continued to believe that everything that had happened in her dreams was real, but as time passed, she started to question her memories. Eventually, all her recollections felt like self-spun fantasies. The reactions of those around her also shaped her thinking.

"I had a dream last night where I met someone I didn't know, and I don't even remember if it was a guy or a girl, but this person was looking at me with so much affection. And I asked what was wrong, and the person said, 'It doesn't matter, you'll forget it anyway.' Isn't that odd? Actually . . . I think I said something more, but it's slipped my mind. But it was a really sweet moment. What kind of dream was that?"

"Forget about it. It's just a silly dream."

This was the standard reaction when people shared their dreams.

"You guys have never had that kind of dream?"

"What, like flying and stuff? I did have a dream once where I was conscious of the fact that I was dreaming. Is that a lucid dream? Se-hwa, have you ever had a lucid dream like that?"

"No. I haven't had a dream in a long time."

Whenever she was asked such a question, Se-hwa wanted to share everything that had happened to her, but she knew no one would believe her, so she just pretended she didn't dream at all.

But, after talking to the student in the counseling

office, she felt compelled to revisit the dream world. She missed the people she'd met there.

Waiting in her car at a red light, Se-hwa looked at the crowd crossing the street and thought to herself, *I wonder if they've had the same experiences as I've had. Is this something that has only happened to me?*

★ ★ ★

After reading the review, Penny rushes straight to Dallergut's office. She knocks on the door but doesn't wait for his answer before flinging it open.

Myers and Dallergut both turn to look at her. Between them is a piece of paper with the complaint on it.

"Dallergut, that complaint is from Customer No. 1, right?"

"Yes," Myers answers her instead. "What brings you in here so urgently?"

Penny cuts to the chase. "How do you and Customer No. 1 know each other, Myers?"

Dallergut and Myers exchange awkward glances.

"I know I may be overstepping . . . But does it have something to do with your college expulsion?" Penny can't help asking.

"That leaves me with no option but to share," Myers says, resigned.

"How about we talk about this another time?" Dallergut interjects.

"No, it's okay. I'm not that naive boy anymore. And I have kept my secret long enough."

Myers starts recounting the story of his college expulsion. Opening up seems to transform him.

". . . That's how I got expelled. I submitted my graduation project without realizing that there was a strict rule—you cannot directly appear in the dreams of out-of-town guests. Even after hearing the whole story, Dallergut still hired me. I didn't find out until later, but he told me that when he heard my story, he immediately realized it had to do with Customer No. 1. Right, Dallergut?"

"It was obvious. As a lucid dreamer she was conspicuous, which likely caught your attention. You were also around the same age."

"So, did you see her again afterward?" Penny is fascinated by his story.

"Yes, not long after I started working on the second floor. I thought I was lucky to see her again so soon, but now, just like any other out-of-town customer, she didn't recognize me."

"How did you deal with that?"

"Of course, I didn't handle it well back then, but I'm okay now. Over the past twenty years, I've come to realize that lucid dreaming doesn't last forever, and I've seen other customers like her. It's not like I'm the only one who went through this, or that there were no other relationships afterward . . . if that makes any difference. I'm just glad that I get to see her as often as I do now. And it's not a bad relationship dynamic— customer and store staff. At least I know she's sleeping well, and that's a lot better than not knowing."

Penny feels sorry for him, but Myers just smiles as if he were recounting a fond memory of an old friend.

"Hearing you recount that story so casually, I feel so guilty, as if I were the bad guy interfering in your relationship with her," says Dallergut.

"Had you not interfered, it would have been a lot harder. It was for the best. She could have wasted a lifetime dreaming, and it would have been much worse. You saved both her and me."

"I notice lately that all she's been paying for her dreams with is Longing. What exactly is her complaint?" Penny asks.

"Would you take a look at this?"

Dallergut hands Penny the piece of paper that has been lying on his desk.

COMPLAINT LEVEL 3: WHEN DREAMING ITSELF BECOMES TOO PAINFUL

Attention: The Dallergut Dream Department Store
Complainant: Regular Customer No. 1
"I'm confused and unsure if my memories are fabri-

cated. Fear and sadness wash over me at the thought that what happened in my past dreams might have all been in my head. And the fact that I can't confirm anything is agonizing. I'm confused every time I dream."

* This is based on the half-asleep complainant's somewhat incoherent account and contains some opinions of the overseeing counselor.

"It makes sense now," says Penny, slapping her knees. "She still misses the time she spent lucid dreaming, and that's why she's been paying with Longing for all the dreams she has had!"

"I guess so. Although I don't know what made her memory come back all of a sudden . . ." Myers is lost in thought.

"Is there anything we can do? I feel so bad for her. If only we could explain . . . It's not fair to leave her thinking it's all her imagination. How frustrating must that be!"

"It's unfortunate, but that doesn't give us the right to create a dream where we appear. We can't break the rules again," says Dallergut, and Myers hangs his head.

"We want to prove that we exist, but we can't even show ourselves in dreams? How can it be possible . . . ?" Penny says, frustrated.

Leaving the discussion open, they each retreat to their

respective desks. The unresolved issue weighs heavily on Penny's mind all day.

***

As Penny walks home from work, all she can think about is Customer No. 1. Taking the longer, slower route on purpose, she stops in front of a billboard bearing the same ad she saw outside the grocery store Adria's Kitchen.

Madam Sage's Mom's Homemade Ketchup and Dad's Homemade Mayonnaise—

Upgraded Version 2021 Now Available
with Deeper Flavors and Emotions
(Contains 0.1 percent Longing)
No Need to Be a Good Cook!
All You Have to Do Is Appeal to Emotions!
Recreate Homemade Flavors
of Your Dear Parents!

Penny's mind immediately turns to Customer No. 1 when she spots the word *Longing* on the ketchup ad. She walks into the grocery store and grabs a bottle of Mom's Homemade Ketchup as she reflects.

How can we let her know her memory is real without making trouble?

She feels the urge to grab anyone walking by and ask for their ideas.

Just then, she catches the back of Assam's head in the large-vat corner ahead. Having a big friend like him is helpful because he stands out in a crowd. Penny quietly sidles up to him.

"Hey, Assam, what are you staring at?"

Unfazed, Assam remains serious, standing in front of a large vat of sauce.

"Penny, look at this. Madam Sage has a new sauce lineup! It's a mustard sauce that will blow your mind."

Assam is pointing to a sign with the tagline *A One-of-a-Kind Mustard Sauce to Clear Your Mind and Your Nose*. It hangs above a row of bright yellow jars. He puts down the mustard sauce and flicks with his front paw at the bottle of "Mom's Handmade Ketchup," which Penny is still holding.

"I'll stick with the classic ketchup," Assam says, "because it can make a sloppy egg dish taste just like my mom's recipe."

"So, a Longing-infused ketchup . . . It won't bring back the memory of someone you've completely forgotten about, will it?"

Penny wants to explain everything to Assam, but she can't just blurt out what Myers has kept secret for so long.

"Don't expect too much from a mere thirty-seal ketchup bottle. By the way, did you hear the news?"

"What news?"

"Yasnoozz Otra might retire."

"Where did you hear that?"

"I have my sources. Apparently, she's seriously think-ing about it. Her dreams aren't selling so well these days, and maybe that made her consider other options."

"No way. She can't! 'Lives of Others' isn't even out yet, let alone its sequel. I'm against this. It would be a waste of her talent."

"I feel the same way. There are so many dreams that only Otra can make," Assam says, as he places a large bottle of Mom's Homemade Ketchup and another of Dad's Homemade Mayonnaise in his cart.

Penny dazedly mutters, "Dreams that only Otra can make . . ." And then a brilliant idea pops into her head as if she'd just eaten a whole bottle of that tangy mustard sauce.

"You're right! This is indeed a dream that only Otra can make. Thank you, Assam!"

Penny glances at her wristwatch as she rushes out of the grocery store.

★ ★ ★

"So, you went to Yasnoozz Otra's mansion by your-self?" Dallergut asks Penny as they display the summer edition "Spooky Dreams" on the first floor. The scary wrapping paper gives a child customer the creeps, and she grabs her mom's hand and quickly rushes past.

"So, you've heard! Yes, I meant to tell you. I thought of a dream for Customer No. 1 and wanted to ask Otra if she could help. Sorry, I was in a hurry."

"No need to be sorry! I heard what dream you asked for. What an amazing idea."

"Do you think I should pursue it?"

"Of course! I'm sure No. 1 will love it. Otra also seems excited to create a fun dream. I haven't seen her so energized in a long time. It's all thanks to you. Can't wait to see it completed."

***

A week later, Yasnoozz Otra shows up at the Dallergut Dream Department Store. She has bags under her eyes from working so hard on the dream, but her hair and clothes are as posh as usual. Otra pulls out a lovely dream box from her handbag.

"I swear, this dream is the best work of my life. I never thought my talent for creating dreams from another person's point of view would be put to such good use! As requested, there is not a single shot of you guys in this dream. Instead, I've captured your diverse perspectives as you look at Customer No. 1. So, I hope that should be okay, Dallergut?" Otra clasps Dallergut's hands, her eyes sparkling with excitement.

"No problem at all. This type of dream is your forte—immersing yourself in someone else's perspective and compressing long periods of time into short dreams. It's a special kind of dream that only you can create, Yasnoozz."

"It was all thanks to Penny's brilliant idea."

Penny blushes at Otra's praise.

Upon hearing the news, Myers and Weather gather at Dallergut's office. Weather even brings No. 1's Eyelid Scale with her as she takes a seat, debating whether or not to stroke it, eager to relay the dream to No. 1 as soon as possible. And just then, the Eyelid Scale flickers.

"Look at this. She is about to fall asleep! I'll go meet her right now!"

Penny sprints to the lobby. Se-hwa has already arrived: she's just in time. Penny escorts her into the office.

Those gathered in the office take a step back, gesturing for Myers to hand the dream box to Se-hwa directly. Myers nervously approaches Se-hwa as she looks around in confusion.

"Why did you bring me here . . . ?" Se-hwa asks.

Myers stiffens and extends the dream box to her without saying a word—but then Otra taps him on the shoulder. "Oh, stop being so stoic. You can do better than that."

Myers contorts his face, summoning a milder expression. "I hope this is the dream you've been looking for."

★ ★ ★

That night, Se-hwa has a dream, a very special one that only Otra could create: "Lives of Others."

In the dream, Se-hwa is a red-haired employee of the Dallergut Dream Department Store—that is, Weather. And, as Weather, she sits still at the front desk, lost in thought about the Eyelid Scales she has developed over the past few months. Not only is Se-hwa a different person in her dream, but she has traveled back in time twenty years. Yet everything she witnesses in her dream is as vivid as if it were right in front of her, and the experience feels so natural that she doesn't perceive it as someone else's perspective.

She catches sight of a woman sneaking around the corner. It isn't the first time this customer has wandered into the department store and tried to escape Weather's notice.

As Weather, she slips out of her seat and follows the customer, who passes Dallergut's office and heads toward the storage room.

That troublemaker is trying to sneak into the dream-payments storage again—good grief!

She chases after the customer in panic, her eyes fixed on the customer's ivory pajamas. Even then, Se-hwa doesn't realize that the customer is her twenty-year-old self.

The scene and point of view shift in an instant, and now she is Dallergut, the owner of the department store.

Dallergut, a young man with black hair, smiles with satisfaction as he places the first Eyelid Scale on the front counter. Then a thought crosses his mind: this eyelid now often remains closed for longer periods of time. He thinks about the owner of the Eyelid Scale, who is freely roaming around the store, oblivious.

Back in his office, Dallergut looks again at the stack of books about lucid dreamers on his desk. As Dallergut, Se-hwa surveys her surroundings, and her gaze lands on a page in the book Dallergut has boldly underlined.

The ability to experience lucid dreaming tends to be more prevalent in childhood or adolescence, with many adept lucid dreamers displaying their skills during these early stages of life. However, maintaining this capability throughout a lifetime is uncommon. As individuals transition into adulthood, most inadvertently lose the proficiency to control their lucid dreams.

And with that, Se-hwa can clearly hear Dallergut's thoughts channeling through her.

She would be devastated if she suddenly lost the ability to have lucid dreams. How should I let her know that she will have a bigger world in real life where she belongs, and that our dream world will always be here for her . . . ? I guess what I can do for now is find a perfect dream for her.

The perspective shifts once more, and she is now Vigo Myers—looking at Se-hwa. Through Myers's eyes, she looks dazzling.

"You know what? Maybe by 2020, two people will be able to have the same dream at the same time! You should make it, Vigo."

"That's a brilliant idea! Will 2020 ever come, though? I mean, I still can't believe 2000 is just around the corner. Where will we be in 2020? I hope I will have become a famous dreammaker by then. Winning an award at the Dream of the Year Awards, you know."

The scene shifts from the café, where they are talking together, to the front of Dallergut's office, where Myers stands. Everything that has crossed Myers's mind—from the moment of Se-hwa's sudden disappearance to his expulsion from college, all the way up to his interview at the dream department store— courses through her.

I shouldn't have asked her to come in normal clothes. That was too selfish of me.

Fast-forward. By some miracle, Myers has been working on the second floor of the department store for a week. His gaze is fixed on a female customer. She doesn't seem to recognize him at all, she just looks at him with the same look that other customers wear. He pushes aside all the words he wants to say and walks up to her.

"Hello. Can I help you with anything?"

***

As soon as Se-hwa wakes up, she opens her phone's notes app. She knows instinctively that this is a dream she must remember.

> In my dream, I saw my past through the eyes of the people I miss. It was the gaze of someone who remembered me. What clearer proof could there be? The dream world definitely exists. I was a killer whale who could return to shore at any time, and I'm sure the people on the shore who miss me know that I'm still swimming diligently in the world where I'm supposed to be. Over the past twenty years, my world has grown deeper and wider, and I have a wide coast to return to every night.

They gave me a dream that I needed, just like they did twenty years ago. Se-hwa is convinced of this. Soon, her dream journal entry fills up her entire screen. She reads it through and, overwhelmed, presses the save button.

***

At the same time, the system beeps at the front desk of the Dallergut Dream Department Store. A huge batch of payments have arrived.

Ding-dong. Payments received from Customer No. 1. A large amount of Affection has been paid for "Lives of Others:

Full Edition." A large amount of Gratitude has been paid for "Lives of Others: Full Edition." A large amount of Happiness has been paid for "Lives of Others: Full Edition." A large amount of Flutter has been paid for "Lives of Others: Full Edition."

FIVE

TACTILE SENSATION OF THE TEST CENTER

Summer is in full glory, with today being the hottest day of the year. The employees of the Dallergut Dream Department Store are all enjoying their lunch break.

Penny decides to have lunch at Chef Grang Bong's restaurant. He is also the creator of "Eating Delicious Food" dreams. She's heard that for this week only, they're offering a special discount on their pizza combo menu, including a coupon for unlimited plum-flavored iced tea if the meal is paid for upfront.

The air-conditioned seats inside the restaurant have been snatched up by early arrivals, leaving Penny to settle for a spot on the terrace with a humid, lukewarm breeze. Her lunchmates are Mogberry and Motail. A backlog of orders has been keeping the trio waiting for their pizza for so long that it feels like the slowest culinary marathon ever.

"By the way, Mogberry. Celine Gluck's Apocalypse

Series is piling up in the discount corner. I keep selling them, but the stock doesn't seem to decrease at all. They just keep accumulating. Can you guys pay more attention on the third floor? I feel like I'm losing my mind selling apocalypse dreams all day."

"Okay, Motail, I get it. I'm fried, too, and I've got an urgent meeting with some dreammakers for the third floor."

"Is your meeting at the Test Center? The container above the Civil Complaint Center? I would love to go see it . . . Can I join?" Motail asks with a sly grin as he leans closer to Mogberry.

"Hey, can you keep a distance when you talk? It's quite stuffy here."

While they talk about work, Penny flips open the latest issue of *Interpretations Better than Dreams*. The sunlight is so bright that she lifts the magazine over her face to create some shade.

When you're shopping dreams for a special occasion, like Christmas or a birthday, go for one of the following, and you'll be praised for your good taste:

1.   a captivating, timeless storyline, like a movie you want to watch over and over

2. a dream customized for each individual
    dreamer
3. fantastical experiences that are only possible
    in dreams

*In early romantic relationships, avoid gifting love dreams,
as they may unfortunately result in the dreamer recalling
their past love.

Penny dog-ears the page for future reference, and
jots down notes before placing the magazine on the
table. A server appears, wiping sweat from his face as
he holds a tray loaded with pizzas, glasses of ice and
a juice jar.

"Pepperoni pizza?" he asks.

"Here," Penny replies, moving her magazine to the
side so the server can place her pizza on the table. As
soon as he sets the juice jar down, Penny pours some
into her glass and gulps it.

"Mind if I take a look?" Motail asks, picking up the
magazine.

"Go ahead."

"Anything interesting?" Mogberry asks, taking a big
bite of her spinach pizza. A few unruly strands of her
loose hair attempt to join the pizza in her mouth.

"Well, not really . . . I mean, it's a daily magazine, you

know. You can't write an interesting story every day . . . Oh, look, everyone, Myers won an award!"

Motail flips open the last page of the magazine and slides it across the table.

Memories Dreams on the Second Floor of the Dallergut Dream Department Store Win the 'Dream with Best Ingredients' in Unanimous 10–0 Vote

Vigo Myers, the manager of the second-floor Memories section, believes the award is a "no-brainer." With no unnecessary additives or stimulating effects, Myers strongly recommends "Memories" dreams for anyone seeking to wake up refreshed . . .

Surprisingly, there is even a photo of a triumphant Myers, with his arms folded. He wears a slight look of disbelief, almost questioning why the award took this long.

"When did he do this interview? Ingredients, additives . . . What's with all these words? Dreams aren't cosmetics." Penny's eyes widen as she shifts her gaze between the article and Mogberry.

"You do know dreammaking requires lots of ingredients, right? Most are necessary for high quality and realistic immersion, but too much of anything can lead to side effects. That's why we test every dream, checking each ingredient before it hits the shelves," Mogberry kindly explains. "When it comes to dreams from the Memories section, though, it's a different story. People's memories can be recreated using a very small amount of ingredients, and the dream can still be as vivid as it was yesterday. And because they're the dreamer's memories, they don't conflict with reality or cause harm. According to the Information Disclosure Act, the memories—"

"Wait, what is the Information Disclosure Act?" Penny interrupts.

"The Information Disclosure Act, enacted in 1995, requires dream product packaging to disclose important information for its consumer, like the ingredients, the dreammaker's name, and the quantity of 101 chemical irritants, in addition to standard information like the product title and expiration date. I mean, the lawmakers behind this must've imagined dream packages stretching about six feet to fit all the disclaimers. And there's an odd exemption: if there's not enough space, you can skip the details and provide them on request. People caught on to this and started coming up with absurdly long product titles just to dodge the need to label irritant chemicals. And guess what? It's a trick still in play today," Mogberry explains in a breathless rant.

"Wow, have you memorized all that?"

"There's a reason why I became the youngest manager."

"Hmm, I don't know. It's hard to grasp just by hearing it. Maybe seeing the ingredients myself could help me understand?" Motail asks Mogberry. But Penny believes he's deliberately feigning ignorance.

"You have a point. Seeing is believing. Very well, I'll let you come with me to the Test Center. You can see some of the dream ingredients there. But take the meeting seriously and don't be a distraction. You'll be there to work, after all, not to tour," Mogberry says sternly.

"Of course! We've been waiting for you to say that." Motail smiles widely, holding his knife and fork.

"If the meeting goes well, we'll have time to browse the ingredients. Actually, there's something you guys can help me with. Speedo asked me to pick up some ingredients for the fourth floor, and it's quite a list."

"I heard they have all the ingredients for the five senses needed to create dreams—so sight, sound, smell, touch, and . . . taste! You can't imagine how long I've been waiting for this day." Motail talks excitedly with his mouth full. A grain of pilaf flies across the table.

"But you're sure you can make it? The meeting's next Wednesday, and it's a fixed schedule with other heads of the dream production companies that can't be changed. They're very busy people," says Mogberry.

"That's the end of the month, so I can definitely make it. I've already hit my sales target for the month. I could take a week off and still be on par with everyone else on the fifth floor. Penny, how about you?"

"I'd love to go, too. Next Wednesday . . . If I get all my work done early, I'm sure Weather will let me go!"

"Great. Just don't push yourself too hard, Penny," Mogberry insists.

"No worries. So, what's the meeting about? Complaints? It looks like there's been quite a few for the third floor," Penny says.

"That's right—and since you guys have already been to the Civil Complaint Center, I guess you're ready for this next step." Mogberry pulls a neatly folded piece of paper out of her pocket and shows it to Penny. "This is what's been driving me crazy lately."

COMPLAINT LEVEL 2: WHEN DREAM AFFECTS DAILY LIFE

Attention: The Dallergut Dream Department Store
CC: Celine Gluck, Chuck Dale, Keith Gruer
* Celine Gluck's "Alien Invasion"
Extreme nervousness caused the complainant to wake up with cold sweats and a headache for fifteen minutes.
* Chuck Dale's "Five Senses of Sensual Dream Series"
Fell out of bed due to overimmersion. Minor bruises occurred.

* Keith Gruer's "Thrilling Bus Ride"
In this dream, the person next to the complainant on
the bus fell asleep, and the complainant leaned their
shoulder, resulting in a sore shoulder and neck upon
waking.

* This report is based on the half-asleep complainant's
somewhat incoherent account and contains some
opinions of the overseeing counselor.

"I sold this customer all those dreams." Mogberry
scratches her head.

"I thought Gluck's End of the World Series was the
only problem. Looks like her other dreams are troublesome as well," Motail says.

"Please don't say that in the meeting. The dreammakers have egos as big as their talent. By the way, Keith
Gruer's 'Thrilling Bus Ride' really worries me. I might
have to stop selling it. Having complaints right out of
the gate is a red flag." Mogberry looks concerned.

* * *

The woman is fast asleep and dreaming.

In her dream, she is on a two-seater bus, traveling
down an unfamiliar road. Her hips ache from the constant road bumps.

But what consumes her mind even more is the man
seated next to her, who is dozing off and leaning on her

shoulder. Though the context is unclear, in her dream, they have just started going out. Were this real life, she would be curious about who he is. But his presence is somehow taken for granted in the dream, with her real-self thoughts intermittently interrupting the dream's flow.

Where is this bus going? I always take the subway, otherwise I get motion sickness . . .

Her thoughts continue to wander, disrupting the dream. Now her mind is flooded with unpleasant memories of an encounter with a stranger on the subway, who also dozed off and left a trail of drool on her shoulder.

Suddenly, she is jolted from distraction, slouching her shoulder to wake the man beside her. But he remains deeply asleep, oblivious to the world. Even asleep, his attractive appearance catches her eye, but she cannot believe how well he is sleeping on someone else's shoulder amid the rattling ride. His audacity feels more shameless than charming.

Throughout that night, the woman dreamed of unwillingly lending her shoulder, and woke up much earlier than she should have. Her right shoulder, which the man had leaned on in the dream, felt stiff and uncomfortable. She couldn't figure out whether her shoulder was hurting because she'd been dreaming about it, or the other way around. She thought about it for a moment, wondering how the complex brain activity of dreaming interacted with her sleeping body, and then she fell back to sleep, unable to resist the overwhelming drowsiness.

* * *

The following Wednesday, Penny leaves the department store refreshed, having finished her work early. The train to the Company District is quiet after rush hour, with only two Noctilucas, Penny, Motail and Mogberry as passengers.

"Mogberry, do you often have meetings with the dreammakers?"

"As often as I eat. I'm probably the most frequent visitor to the Company District from our store. I love the dynamic dreams on the third floor, but they're a lot of work, and I have to keep the tactile levels in check . . ." Mogberry, sitting next to Penny, sighs heavily.

"Tactile levels?" Penny asks.

"Hmm . . . How should I explain this? Well, let's say you're in a dream and you're shot by an enemy. If you wake up and the spot where you were shot in the dream still feels painful, would you want to buy such a scary dream?"

Penny shakes her head.

"That's why we have to weaken tactile sensations

like pain. The magnitude of the sensations in a dream doesn't have to be the same as in real life. In fact, it often shouldn't be, at least for the tactile sensations. But the dreammakers crank the tactile levels up a little bit because they want to make it feel realistic. Because of this we have a regulation that limits tactile sensation levels, whether it's pressure or nociception. It's a special law by the Civil Complaint Center, and it's still being enforced. In the old days, Keith Gruer's 'Thrilling Bus Ride' would have been classified as a level-one complaint, not a level two," says Mogberry, wiping sweat from the bridge of her nose with a handkerchief. "By the way, it's really hot today. I hope the train breezes down Dizzying Downhill."

Apparently, the driver shares the sentiment, applying less Rebellious than usual for the downhill stretch. The train speeds up as they descend, offering a thrilling ride with excited screams from Penny and the others, as well as grumbles from the Noctilucas, who complain that this could have blown away their laundry.

The Noctilucas disembark at the Noctiluca Laundry stop, leaving only three passengers on the train: Penny, Motail and Mogberry. The stall owner holds up an energy drink, half-heartedly trying to sell it, but Penny vigorously shakes her head no.

"You're welcome to take the leftover newspaper for

free," says the stall owner as if he is doing them a huge favor, tossing the papers into the train. A meal plan, useless now that it's after lunchtime, falls among the papers, along with an insert the size of a palm. A gorgeous red glossy advertising flyer:

Introducing Our Snowflake Ice
Cream with Thirty Emotions!
Fortune Cookies Also Available to Transform
Your Life (First Come, First Served)
"Don't miss the red ice-cream truck—
it will appear before you know it!"

"What is that?" Motail and Mogberry both ask Penny as she picks up the flyer that fell at her feet.

"It's just one of those generic ads. I guess the weekly lunch menus weren't enough to sell the papers, so now they're taking ads."

***

After a short ascent up the hill to the Company District, the three head straight to the Test Center, located on top of the trunklike Civil Complaint Center. The complaint center, as well as the Central Square, is quieter than when they came here with Dallergut. Everyone seems to be inside the building, probably because it is business hours.

They take the elevator from the Civil Complaint Center on the first floor to the second floor, which is full of green plants.

An employee greets them. "Welcome to the Test Center. Let me check your badges."

The three hold out the badges hanging from their necks.

"Confirmed, thank you. Have you been to the Test Center before? If you need directions, we can help you."

"No need. I've been here before," says Mogberry.

"Very well. We have staff in every section, so if you have any questions, feel free to ask. All ingredients must be paid for at the till by the entrance, and then you can use them in here or take them outside. Please note that the hearing workrooms are already booked for the entire week."

The Test Center has a complex interior structure: what appears to be a stack of containers from the outside is actually a three-story space connected by a staircase.

Mogberry gestures to the different spaces. "There are dedicated areas for the senses of sight, smell, touch, taste and hearing, and a miscellaneous area. You'll need different ingredients depending on which sense you're testing in your dreams. Each area has its own workroom, which can be used by reservation only. The auditory test room is always competitive."

Penny realizes that each of the colorful containers visible from outside is a separate space dedicated to a specific sensory theme.

"Look, Penny. Isn't that a great idea? We should incorporate something similar in our store." Motail taps Penny and points to a corner.

Numerous pulleys are silently circling up and down the stairs to transport goods in large buckets—from the first to third floor, the third to second floor, and the second to first floor.

Just opposite the entrance stands a grand slide. A woman glides down it from the third floor to the first. She lands smoothly, dusts off her pants, and casually walks away.

"My friends said they booked the workroom closest to the tactile corner for us. Let's go."

Mogberry leads the way. "If you go through the olfactory corner here and then through the visual corner, you get to the tactile corner."

Penny's nose is getting overstimulated from all the different smells coming out of the olfactory corner. Motail stops and sniffs at scent kits, organized by type on a rotating shelf.

"Scent kits are great for beginner dreammakers," Mogberry says. "When you're new to creating backgrounds, it's much more effective to conjure up a setting in the dreamer's head through scent, and there's nothing like a familiar scent to trigger memories."

"Yeah, I have quite a few memories that come back when I smell certain scents," Penny says.

Two young dreammakers, no older than Penny, are standing in front of the various branded scent kits, comparing and debating which to buy. They've dug into pockets for their money, and are counting it in their palms.

"I want to buy the recipe book too, but I'm thirty seals short . . ." One of them sulks.

Next to them is an employee in charge of the smell corner.

"We're giving out recipes for a few signature scents if you purchase a scent kit. They include the aroma of rice being cooked, the scent of ink from the newspaper, and the briny tang of the fish market. Nostalgic scents vary depending on the cultural characteristics of the customer, so it's important to first decide on the kind of customer you're creating a dream for." He seems excited to find novices to whom he can show off his hard-earned knowledge, something he rarely gets to do because he usually interacts with veteran dreammakers.

"See those round tents in the middle that look like igloos?" Mogberry asks as they walk past them.

"Are they workrooms?"

"Yes. If the entrance is zipped closed, it means they're in use, so don't go into one of those."

A few of the tents, however, are unzipped. The three walk quietly, trying not to make any sounds with their steps.

"It's like a giant indoor campground," Motail says. This isn't just because of the tepeelike appearance of the workrooms: most people in the vicinity are dressed in tracksuits or outdoor clothing. Penny worries that some of these employees might have been working for days without going home.

The three walk up the staircase past the olfactory corner and into the next space. Even the space next to the stairs is put to use for displaying goods.

Penny cannot take her eyes off the huge palette of colors on display. "Wow, it's a palette of 36,000 all-natural colors!"

"Yes. We're now in the visual corner. You can make almost any color with that palette. But it's expensive, and very few people know how to use it well. I don't think anyone but Wawa Sleepland buys them these days," Mogberry notes. Penny walks slowly, with her eyes fixed on the palette.

After the palette, she notes a series of sample background chunks. The round, claylike lumps of mixed colors are packaged individually, each chunk nestled within its own container. Adjacent to the displayed products sits a clear acrylic container the size of a large moving box, along with a sign. Inside the acrylic box is a lonely unlit lantern.

> Place your choice of background
> chunk under the light source,
> and the background will come
> alive! Try before you buy!

"This sample *background chunk* can create an optical illusion in a small space around you if it interacts with the right amount of light. It's not directly used to create dreams, but many use it to train newbie dreammakers, or as a sample for production meetings," Mogberry explains as she takes the lid off the acrylic box. She slides one free trial background chunk through the hole in the lantern. As soon as she turns on the lantern, the background chunk, which is marine blue with yellow and red patches, shrinks. At the same time, background color blots gradually spread around the lantern, and before long, the acrylic box is colored like a night sky above the seashore, with yellow and red firecrackers bursting against a deep ultramarine blue background. Motail and Penny cling to the box and exclaim.

"Don't look too closely. It'll hurt your eyes," Mogberry warns.

Penny wants to take her time exploring all the sensory corners, but the taste, hearing and miscellaneous senses are at the opposite end.

The moment the three arrive at the tactile corner, a woman in front of a tent notices Mogberry and waves cheerfully. She sports snug, cushioned slippers, and her hair is haphazardly rolled into a high bun.

"There you are!" Mogberry greets her.

"Welcome, Mogberry! Thank you for coming all this way."

"Guys, this is Celine Gluck. Celine, this is Penny and Motail from our store."

"Hello. I'm Penny. I work at the front desk on the first floor of the Dallergut Dream Department Store."

"I'm Motail. I work on the fifth floor."

"Welcome. Let's head inside. Chuck Dale and Keith Gruer should be here any minute now, so let's go in first and wait for them."

Up close, Celine Gluck appears fatigued, like she's been awake for three straight nights. Her slippers emit a soft, airy sound with each step.

Inside, the tent is impeccably neat and organized. Besides the typical video equipment and a few crude, unidentifiable gadgets, there is no clutter. It is spacious enough to fit about ten people and is made of taut white material.

"Celine, have you been sleeping in your studio again? Don't strain yourself." Mogberry looks at Celine Gluck, worried.

"Well, I've been hung up on my new project. While we wait for the other two dreammakers, can you maybe take a look at it, Mogberry? I want to hear your honest opinion. You two as well, please." Celine Gluck pulls a background chunk from a locked box. She holds it to a lantern in the center of the tent. "Okay, this is the first candidate for my new release. The story should be self-explanatory."

As soon as Gluck operates the remote control, the background chunk begins to melt away, painting the white tent with a multitude of colors. Then, for a moment, the tent turns pitch-black. Suddenly, Penny hears the clinking sound of bullets being loaded. Flashes of light pass by in front of her eyes, like shadows of people trying to investigate the dark room from outside. Then she hears a booming voice—"Found them!"—followed by the appearance of a swarm of riot police with guns drawn.

Penny knows this is all just a visual illusion, but her body ducks under the desk to hide. Motail and Mogberry sit still, looking unfazed.

"What do you all think?" Celine Gluck looks at the three.

"The high stakes in an enemy-infested village . . . The shadows of the enemies reflected outside the window. The cold sweat and the suffocating tension at the climax just before you wake up to reality . . . This is almost exactly the same as what was released in the first quarter of last year, only it's been switched from aliens to SWAT teams . . . I've got a ton of dreams like this on the fifth floor. And for the record, the fifth floor sells leftover dreams from other floors for clearance."

Shocked by Motail's cutting critique, Celine Gluck twirls the ballpoint pen in her hand. Apparently, nobody else around her has been this frank.

"W-well, then how about this other one?" Celine Gluck takes another chunk from the box, places it inside the lantern, and fiddles with the remote control.

Once again, the inside of the tent turns black as the night sky, and a fiery meteorite flies straight toward the workroom. The sound of the earth rumbling is so real that Penny wonders if she should evacuate, but she tries to keep her outward appearance calm. Amid the commotion, Mogberry is calmly observing, scribbling notes on a piece of paper, and Motail's lips twitch as if he's ready to tear it apart with his critique again.

"What do you think?" Celine Gluck asks, this time turning to Penny.

"The visuals are wonderful," Penny says honestly.

"Really? Thanks, Penny!"

"But we've already seen this, too," Motail chimes in. "The only update is visual quality. I can see this on the fifth floor already . . ."

Penny pokes Motail in the side. Crestfallen, Celine Gluck pulls the background chunk out of the lantern and tucks it back inside the box. Suddenly, the tent turns back to white.

"What do you think is the problem?" Gluck asks.

"I think there's too much emphasis on creating tension," Mogberry suggests as she diligently refers to the notes she's made, providing a rational critique. "Of course, all your work at Celine Gluck Films is wonderful, but these days, there is a high demand for dreams that offer the thrill of a dangerous escape. Our customers on the third floor look for dreams that can fulfill their heroism or give them a sense of exhilaration, like when you play a video game."

Just then, a little bell hanging outside the tent rattles.

"Sounds like they're finally here." Celine Gluck stands up as two men appear through the tent entrance.

"Hello. Hope we're not too late!"

Keith Gruer keeps a short hairstyle, as he shaves his head after every breakup. Next to him is a man with neatly trimmed shoulder-length hair.

"Hello, Mogberry. I see some new faces from the

dream department store. I'm Chuck Dale. I create erotic dreams. My notable work is the Five Senses of Sensual Dream Series."

Unbeknownst to themselves, Penny and Motail each release a deep, low moan. It may not be as loud as a thunderous ovation, but it is loud enough to convey *I'm a fan of yours!*

Chuck Dale responds with a contented grin.

"Well, I prefer to incorporate platonic love into my work, unlike this guy," Keith Gruer chimes in. "We live in a world where spiritual love has been so devalued, but I still look for a higher dimension of love . . ."

"Which is why your hair has no time to grow because you're looking for dimensions in love," remarks Chuck Dale, running his hand through his own hair as if to show off.

"Anyway, Mogberry, I know you have something to tell me. And I think I know what it is." Keith Gruer is one jump ahead of Mogberry before she can speak.

"Well, great. That makes it easier for us to talk. We're going to have to recall all stocks for 'Thrilling Bus Ride.'"

"I see. Is there no other option on the table?" Keith asks bitterly as he takes a seat.

"How about we sit down and talk it through?"

"That would be great, since the three of us all have a similar working process."

"The three of you share a similar process? Your work is so different," Motail says.

"We're similar in that our focus is on tactile sensations. We dreammakers usually identify our strong suit before our debut," says Chuck Dale.

"In dreams, balancing all five senses equally is impossible because there's constant interaction with the dreamer's actual senses. So most dreammakers emphasize a specific sense instead and find better success that way. The renowned dreammakers, the so-called Legendary Big Five, are famous precisely because they excel in all sensory aspects," Keith Gruer adds.

"As far as the tactile sense goes, we three are definitely at the top tier," Celine Gluck says. Penny deeply admires her confidence.

"That is exactly what I'm getting at," Mogberry says professionally. "You all might want to focus on the specific tactile sense and drastically cut back on the setup. I think part of the problem with your dreams is the sensory overload. You don't really need all those other senses—they actually get in the way and make the experience less immersive, leaving you distracted by things like unnecessary shoulder pain. The tactile sense itself is low enough and is not a problem."

"So, let the memories in the dreamer's head be the natural backdrop instead of enforcing superficial backgrounds?"

"Yes, exactly."

"Well, I guess that makes a lot of sense. The memories, if done right, can create a lot of resonance. We'd get a lot of Excitement for payment. And you're saying trying to force the background like we do now could backfire. Not everyone can create a perfect background like Wawa Sleepland." Chuck Dale agrees with Mogberry.

"Yeah. Well, if that's the consensus here . . ." Keith Gruer looks to Penny and Motail and asks, "Can I run a little test? Since we have two perfect testers here."

"I brought my sample, too," Chuck Dale adds, pulling a box out of his pocket.

"Testers . . . Meaning us?" Penny asks.

"Yes. Chuck, can I go first?"

"Absolutely."

Keith Gruer stands up and puts a background chunk into the lantern. The chunk has no color or pattern. When he turns on the lantern, nothing happens, unlike Celine Gluck's sample.

"I want you two to gently touch the tips of your index fingers together."

Penny and Motail hesitate, then comply with Keith's request, touching their fingertips. A thrill runs through their hands and spreads down their bodies. Penny's fingertips tingle and flutter, like that time she accidentally touched the fingertips of the boy sitting next to her at school, and she feels a ridiculous urge to hold Motail's hand.

Motail seems to feel the same thing, and he jumps out of his chair, shivering. "What are you doing?" he screams at Penny.

"I didn't do anything. What were *you* trying to do?"

"I'm sorry, guys. It's not your fault. It's all because I'm too good." Keith Gruer caresses his shaved head, flustered. "So, what kind of background did you two recall?"

Penny regains her composure and answers, "I imagined a classroom from my school days."

"Really? Mine was my go-to diner." Motail looks at Penny wide-eyed and then at Keith Gruer.

"Wonderful. It proves successful. So we don't have to worry about creating backdrops if the dreamer comes up with the right one on their own."

"This is incredible. How can a single touch of the fingertip trigger different memories?" Motail seems to have a newfound respect for Keith Gruer.

"That's because you carry a treasure trove of wonderful memories within you, whether from actual experiences or from movies and TV shows. With the right stimulus, they can transform into the backdrop for a delightful dream, with a trigger as simple as the touch of your fingertips or a particular scent and sound."

Penny finds it fascinating that she has a reservoir of memories she can draw upon for her dream backdrops anytime. Such an idea never occurred to her.

"Very well. Now, shall we move on to mine? Again, just a fingertip would do." Chuck Dale puts his sample into the lantern.

Motail and Penny reach out their fingers, but just before they touch, Penny remembers: Chuck Dale creates erotic dreams. She presses her finger against Motail, desperately praying that her feared scenario will not come to pass.

A tingle starting from her fingertip spreads up her elbow and through her body, and Penny feels a rush of emotion that terrifies her. Though she's making the same gesture as before, it feels completely different. It's the kind of intense emotion that feels like it could lead to a spontaneous kiss, and Penny almost runs out of the tent. The same sickened look spreads across Motail's face as he once again jumps out of his chair in shock.

"Looks like I haven't lost my touch," Chuck Dale says with satisfaction.

"Never, ever put us through something like that again, please," Motail replies, his face flushing red in apparent disgust.

For the rest of the day, the three dreammakers and Mogberry delve into topics such as how to embody the balance of the five senses and how to manipulate the passage of time. Penny pinches her thigh, desperately trying to stay awake amid the maelstrom of complicated discussions.

"All right, then. I'll take this sample to Dallergut for a report," Mogberry says, grabbing the sample. As she stands up, the screeching sound of her chair scraping against the floor startles Penny out of her daze.

"We're done?" Motail asks languidly as he scratches the back of his neck. It is obvious that he dozed off as well.

"Ugh. You kept nodding off, didn't you?"

"No, I didn't. I was paying attention."

"You're lying. Tell me, what have the three dream-makers decided to work on for their new title? If you were actually paying attention, you'll know."

"Uh, well . . . Since they are making it together, it's going to be sensual, emotional and spectacular . . . Just the whole package. So, a dream where you embark on a high-stakes adventure with your crush, set in a war-torn state where romance unfolds, and it concludes with a passionate kiss?"

Judging by Mogberry's startled expression, Motail has nailed it. "You're lucky," Mogberry says.

"Anyway, we should probably get back to work. I'm so tired." Celine Gluck stands up, yawning.

"And we should get those ingredients Speedo asked for and return to the store," Mogberry says to Penny and Motail as she packs her purse.

The two groups walk out of the tent and go their separate ways.

"Now, we need to buy the sensory ingredients listed here," Mogberry says. "The sensory corners are all scattered, so let's each target one section and pick them up. If you can't find them, just ask around. They have staff on every corner."

Mogberry jots down the items on two pieces of paper and hands one to Penny and the other to Motail. "Meet me at the checkout by the entrance when you're done!"

Even at a glance, it is clear that Mogberry has assigned more items to the two of them than are on her own list. But before they can complain, Mogberry waves and disappears among the tents.

"I'm going up there." Motail points to the topmost floor, where the hearing corner is located. "Maybe I can try the slide on the way down . . ."

"Okay, I'll head over to the miscellaneous corner, then. See you in a bit." Penny shuffles off.

★ ★ ★

The miscellaneous corner turns out to be the kind of place Motail would have loved. It exudes a free-spirited vibe similar to that of the fifth floor at the

Dallergut Dream Department Store, but there appear to be far too few staffers compared to the number of customers. It seems like she'll need to find her own ingredients. Penny grabs one of the yellow shopping baskets and explores the shelves. Her eyes widen like those of a pirate spotting treasure. Standing beneath precariously arranged stacks of tools, she looks at the list Mogberry assigned, trying to stay focused.

"Let's see. A dozen Fresh Peppermint and two sets of Shifting Gravity."

After passing some musty-smelling baskets and a line of unidentified wheelbarrows, Penny finally finds what she needs. Known for its invigorating effects after sleep, Fresh Peppermint has a caveat that it should be used only for nap dreams that last less than thirty minutes. Shifting Gravity comes with pages of instructions.

Shifting Gravity can serve as an effective sleep alarm for a quick doze, but it comes with side effects, including uncontrollable noises, mild bruising or, depending on your sleeping location, serious injury. It's not advised for elderly or those with disabilities. Additionally, please adhere to the recommended allowance.

Among the other items on display, there's Sharpening Pigmentation, powerful enough to change the color of an entire bucket of water with just one drop. Next to it is Sucking Pipette, which is a tool designed for extracting incorrect colors or ingredients. Penny finds a Leprechaun grunting in front of the neatly organized pipette display. The Leprechaun attempts to press down on the pipette's rubberized handle with all his power, but when he can't get it to work, he fusses with the employee.

"You need to make a smaller one! Forget about the old saying that a craftsman doesn't blame his tools!"

Penny walks past the Leprechaun, eyeing him anxiously, wondering whether he will drop the glass pipette on the floor. Sure enough, she soon hears a loud clatter coming from the Leprechaun's direction. She moves away from the commotion, delving deeper into the Test Center.

Penny's looking for a cassette tape called White Noise for Sleep. It sounds like it would be in the hearing corner, but Mogberry's note indicates that it's in the miscellaneous corner. She stumbles upon a box full of cassette tapes on the lowest shelf and can't help but let out a delighted squeal.

Penny tosses White Noise for Sleep into her basket and is just standing up to leave when she spots some familiar faces across the aisle. It's Kick Slumber and Animora Bancho, both of whom specialize in animal-related dreams. They seem to have just bumped into each other and don't notice Penny.

"Hey, Bancho, what did you buy so many ingredients for?" Slumber asks Bancho, whose hands are full of shopping.

"Hey, Slumber, how's it going? I rarely get down from the mountains, so I figured I'd stock up. If it weren't for the Bestseller prize I won last year, I wouldn't be able to shop this generously." Bancho smiles heartily.

"Are those lenses new?" Slumber asks, lifting a crutch to point at something that's hard to see from Penny's position.

"Oh, these are called Frog Lenses. I haven't tried one myself, but it's a lens that can give you the vision of a frog. You should give it a shot, Slumber. You make dreams of becoming an animal."

"Well, if it's in a frog's vision, everything will look gray. It won't be useful for people who want to dream about becoming a frog."

"How so?"

"They'll be too distracted, wondering why everything looks so gray. What they want to experience from becoming a frog is leaping with their hind legs and exploring freely both on land and in water."

"That's a good point. In my case, as a human who recreates the experiences of animals, I focus on the very essence of animalistic sensations. You seem to lean toward the transcendental qualities that people commonly perceive from animals, accentuating these qualities instead of replicating the true sensations animals experience. I thought our dreams were similar, but I now realize I was mistaken."

Penny, not wanting to interrupt their engrossing work conversation, quietly moves toward the other side of the room. She notices some colorful powders, each in its own sack. She walks up to a staffer. "What are these?"

"They're Emotion Powders," the employee replies as he struggles to pick up a sack that has fallen to one side.

"They're emotions in powdered form?"

"Yes. Emotion Powder is much more concentrated than its original form. It's specifically designed for dreammaking because it's easier to control than its liquid form. You can scoop as much as you want into this bag here with a teaspoon. Of course, the price per gram varies from emotion to emotion."

Penny feels a sense of nostalgia, remembering weekend outings to the farmers market with her parents during her childhood, cherished memories of selecting fresh produce and weighing it on the scales.

She wanders around until she comes to the sparse, eerie area where negative Emotion Powders are located. Just as she's about to turn around, she hears whispers in the corner. There are people talking in low voices in front of a crimson-colored sack of Guilt powder, and they look familiar. It's Maxim, the nightmare dream-maker, and Nicholas, also known as Santa Claus.

"I'm glad Guilt is still cheap. We need, like, a lot," Maxim whispers.

"I know. I didn't expect the business to do so well. Maxim, you're so much like Atlas, and yet so different. But I like you much better." Nicholas chuckles as he gives Maxim a loud slap on the back.

Atlas? Penny has heard that name before, but she can't recall where. Afraid she might seem like she's eavesdropping, Penny purposely rustles a sack of emotion next to her to make her presence known.

"Wow, what a pleasant surprise to see you guys here," she says, awkwardly.

Maxim is so surprised to run into Penny that he spills his Guilt all over the floor. Without thinking, he bends down and starts sweeping up the powder with his bare hands—which, of course, overwhelms him with guilt.

"Oh, no. I should've been more careful. It's all my fault. I'm so irredeemably stupid," Maxim says, clutching his head as if in agony, and Penny doesn't know what to do.

"Oh, no . . . By the way, what's all this Guilt for?" Penny asks.

"Well, that's . . . a trade secret. I'm sorry." At Penny's

offhand question, Maxim seems painfully torn between his desire to tell her and the secret he has to keep.

"It's okay if you don't want to tell me. I'm sure you need it for your new production. But first, let's clean up the spill."

"As long as you wear a mask and gloves when you deal with Emotion Powder like this, it should be okay." Nicholas deftly moves the self-pitying Maxim aside. He puts on a disposable mask and bends down to pick up the spilled Guilt powder. Penny quickly grabs another pair of gloves lying by the sacks and bends down to help.

As Nicholas stoops, a wad of paper falls out from his vest pocket.

> Introducing Our Snowflake Ice
> Cream with Thirty Emotions!
> Fortune Cookies Also Available to Transform
> Your Life (First Come, First Served)
> "Don't miss the red ice-cream truck—
> it will appear before you know it!"

Nicholas hurriedly snatches up the wad, shoves it into his pocket, and lets out a nervous cough. He glances over to see if Penny noticed. The act is suspicious, but she pretends she hasn't seen anything. Yet these flyers are definitely the same as the one she saw earlier at the stall, tucked inside the free newspaper.

"By the way . . . What brings you here, Penny?" Nicholas asks.

"I'm here on an errand to buy some ingredients. I didn't mean to interrupt. Oops, I'm going to be late. It was nice running into you." Penny hurries out, thinking Mogberry and Motail might be waiting for her.

As expected, Mogberry is already waiting at the entrance.

"Motail's not done yet?" Penny asks.

"Nope, he's still over there."

Mogberry points to the slide. An excited Motail is sliding down it, both hands in the air.

"Motail, enough! That's the fifth time already," Mogberry shouts.

Grinning, Motail returns to Penny and Mogberry. "This is such a fun place! What took you so long, Penny?"

"It took me a while to find my stuff—and actually, I ran into Nicholas and Maxim."

"Nicholas? I thought he stays in his cabin in the snowy mountains during the offseason." Motail pulls down the hems of his pants, which rolled up when he went down the slide.

"What does he do during the offseason, Mogberry?

He seems to be working on something with Maxim. I wonder if they're making new dreams or something. Do you know what he's been up to?"

"No idea. I do hear that Nicholas has been coming to town a lot lately, but I don't know what he's doing with Maxim."

"Well, I didn't have the chance to ask that, but maybe I should have, since he was buying tons of Guilt powder," Penny says curiously.

"Guilt powder? What on earth could it be for?" Mogberry wonders.

"It's a good powder for Maxim's field. Maybe he's trying to create scarier nightmares this year. But the collaboration between a nightmare dreammaker like Maxim and Santa Claus, who works on kids' dreams, does seem odd . . . Does that mean Santa Claus has developed a taste for tormenting children?" Motail says jokingly.

"No way!" Penny wishes she had asked Maxim more when she had the chance.

SIX

SANTA CLAUS IN DOWNTIME

Penny sleeps in the next day. The weather is still hot and humid. She races from home, but soon she's sweating, so she slows down. She won't have time to read *Interpretations Better than Dreams* in the storage room today, but even moving at a slower pace, she'll still get to work on time.

The grounds of the shopping district streets are clean, devoid of any dirty footprints or litter. But the walls surrounding the Leprechauns' shoe shop and nearby telephone poles are covered in flyers and assorted advertisement posters, creating a disorderly appearance. A crowd of people in pajamas gather around one of the ads, and Penny stands on tiptoes behind them to catch a glimpse.

Introducing Our Snowflake Ice
Cream with Thirty Emotions!

Fortune Cookies Also Available to
Transform Your Life (First Come, First Served)
"Don't miss the red ice-cream truck—
it will appear before you know it!"

It's the flyer that slipped out of Nicholas's pocket at the Test Center. Did Nicholas put all this up? Why did he suddenly decide to get into the business of selling food? And the flyer is placed exactly at adult eye level. The fact that this ice-cream ad, something that would usually be meant for kids, is positioned in this way bothers Penny. Anyone else might have overlooked it, but Nicholas, with his marketing expertise, wouldn't have missed such a detail.

Penny glances around but doesn't see a red food truck that could be selling these treats. She thinks for a second, then turns to leave, beads of sweat trickling down the back of her neck. *Forget about the snowflake ice cream*, Penny tells herself. Soon she'll get to the department store and into the cool air-conditioning. She can't wait.

But when she arrives, the department store is not as cool as Penny expected. Weather is already there at the front desk.

"Weather, is the air-conditioning broken or something?" Penny asks as Weather, hair in a tight ponytail, fans herself.

"Yes. Apparently, it broke down last night. A repair-man is supposed to be here this afternoon, but until then, we just have to leave the doors wide open to let some air in. I'm worried about the customers."

"Oh, no. I'll completely melt before the end of the day."

"Let's turn up the ceiling fans to the max. By the way, the Civil Complaint Center called us to ask for a brief confirmation that the complaints we brought in are resolved. I've told the floor managers to get the paperwork together. They should be done by now. Would you mind stopping by each floor this morning to collect the paperwork? I have some off-site work to do."

"Sure. Where're you going?"

". . . To the bank. I need to drop off dream payments," Weather says, pretending she doesn't see Penny, who is sweating profusely.

"So you're going to the bank . . . where they defi-nitely have working air-conditioning . . ."

"Don't look at me like that, Penny. I'm not going to the bank because of the air-conditioning. I have a lot of dream money to deposit today." Weather walks out with light steps.

Penny decides to pick up the paperwork on each floor before the store gets more crowded. There were no complaints about the second floor, so she heads straight to the third.

"Here you go, Penny," says Mogberry, handing over
several pages of paperwork. "These were all the complaints from our floor. They've all been either resolved
or addressed, and I've thoroughly outlined which actions were taken. This should be sufficient for the
Civil Complaint Center." The paperwork is organized
with color-coordinated paper clips and annotated with
matching highlighters. Such a Mogberry thing to do.
Penny chuckles.

Speedo from the fourth floor also has his documents
in perfect order. "I finished them long ago, on the day
Weather asked me. What took you so long to collect
them?"

"Well, you could have brought them to the front desk
yourself . . . What about that other stack you're holding?
They're not for me?"

"These are mine for safekeeping. I need to start preparing for next year's salary negotiation. Always keep a
copy with you, Penny."

Finally, on the fifth floor, Penny catches the first employee she sees and says, "I'm here to pick up complaints
for the Civil Complaint Center," but the employee won't
look her in the eye—and neither will Motail.

"You're not done yet?" Penny raises her voice, a bit
agitated, and the other employees playfully push Motail
forward.

"Penny, look at us," Motail says. "As you can see, we simply do not have the luxury of caring about such trivial stuff. I've said it before, and I'll say it again. I don't understand the complaints for the fifth floor. This is a discount section, after all! We're selling it cheap *because* it's flawed. Cut me some slack. Plus, I'm bad at paperwork."

For the first time, Penny realizes that there actually is an area in which Motail is not confident.

"You know, Motail, you're right. It seems to me the fifth floor does need a manager."

★ ★ ★

Back at the front desk, Penny is organizing all the complaints for the last time when she realizes something: in addition to each of the complainants, there are two other regulars who have recently stopped coming in: Customers No. 330 and No. 620. But she can't find any record of complaints from them, even after rubbing her eyes and searching again. They seem to have stopped coming in without any explanation.

Penny fans herself with one hand and opens the Dream Pay Systems window with the other. The ceiling fans are cranked up to their strongest setting, but that isn't enough to combat the sweltering heat.

It is so humid that Penny can barely focus on the

information she's pulled up about Customers No. 330 and No. 620. She stands up to get some ice water from the staff lounge—and suddenly, the customers in the lobby rush out of the store, pointing across the street.

"Look, there's a red truck!"

"The red truck from that ad? Do they sell snowflake ice cream?"

Sure enough, a red ice-ream truck has pulled up in front of the bank.

"What's all this fuss about?" Weather, who has just returned from her trip to make a deposit, observes the spectacle of people blocking the bank in disbelief.

As soon as she goes on her lunch break, Penny sprints toward the red truck. She doesn't feel like eating in the scorching heat. All she wants is something cold. There are still a lot of people near the crosswalk, at least twice the usual crowd.

Amid the smells of all the hot food from the other food trucks, including the boiling onion milk, this red food truck is the only one emitting any cool air. Other food-truck owners get out of their trucks and keep glancing at the red one. The owner of the onion milk stall glares as he stirs an unsold batch, which has been simmering for so long that it sticks to the bottom of the pot and smells funky.

As Penny joins the back of the long line, she recognizes the two men in the truck. They are, indeed, Nicholas and Maxim. Nicholas is frantically scooping ice cream into round crystal glasses and handing them to customers. With his short white hair, long white beard and an even whiter apron, he looks like a snowman come to life.

"Two ice creams laced with Thrill, right?" he says to his customer.

A student takes the deep blue snowflake ice creams, which look fluffy like snow, and walks past Penny. After taking a quick photo of the ice cream, he takes a bite. "Wow, this tastes so good!" the student marvels, shivering all over.

Inside the red truck, Penny can see a beverage refrigerator stocked with frosty sparkling soda that reads *17 percent Freshness Added*. She recalls having tried this at Nicholas's cabin. He must have brought them down from the Million-Year Snow Mountain.

Maxim, on the other hand, stands solemnly by the oven inside the red truck, his black apron caked with flour. He pulls a golden, flaky sheet of cookie dough out of the oven and swiftly folds a long piece of paper over it, moving with a skill that suggests he's been in the game for a while.

"What is he making?" people ask one another as they watch Maxim.

"Thank you all for waiting. We have free fortune cookies for you all—first come, first served!"

Next to a tray full of fortune cookies, Maxim sets up a large sign:

**Pick a Fortune Cookie and Welcome
Positive Change into Your Life**
The more you eat, the greater the effect,
but please take only one so that
everyone else gets their share.
(And keep the message inside the
fortune cookie to yourself!)

People who've already picked up their ice creams start taking a fortune cookie each as they leave. Penny wants to grab one as soon as possible, but doesn't want to lose her place in the ice-cream line. She's counting how many people are ahead of her when she recognizes a customer right in front of her.

"Dallergut!" Penny calls out, as Dallergut receives his green ice cream and makes his way over. To her disappointment, he doesn't have a fortune cookie with him.

"Penny, this ice cream is really good! But this bright red truck—isn't it obvious whose taste it is?"

"I had no idea that Nicholas and Maxim had started a

new business! Why didn't you take one of those fortune cookies? They're free! I'm going to try one."

"Penny, if you eat a free cookie that Nicholas gives away, you should be prepared to get out of bed on the wrong side, especially if it's a cookie he and Maxim made together . . . You have been warned," Dallergut says enigmatically.

∗ ∗ ∗

Inside an apartment complex, a young couple and a boy carrying a cat carrier were going up in an elevator. The couple peeked inside the crate the boy was holding.

"That's a very cute one."

"Do you like cats?" the boy asked.

"Of course. They're such adorable creatures, but we never got the chance to have one. Thought it'd be better not to bring one home unless we were sure we could take good care of it," the wife said gently.

"That's right. My mom says you have to be really responsible if you want to have a pet. We actually got our cat from a shelter. The previous owner must have abandoned it."

"Poor thing! How could anyone do that?" the wife exclaimed.

"I know, right? I wish there were more people like you two. Oh, I'm getting off here. Bye-bye!"

After the boy got off, the couple exchanged a know-ing chuckle.

"His parents must have their hands full—a child and a cat," the wife said.

"Poor thing! How could anyone do that?" The man teased as he mimicked what she had just said.

"Stop it," the wife snapped. "You know we had our reasons."

"You're right. How on earth were we supposed to know that we had allergies to cat fur?"

"We had no idea."

The two were a match made in heaven, acting and thinking alike. They had got a cat on impulse in their old house, and before they'd moved into their current apartment, they had abandoned it on the street without any guilt, thinking they were returning it back to nature. The sight of the cat staring back at them expectantly from across the street was etched in their memory.

In fact, for the couple, everything came with excuses. Whether it was because they came from a poor family, or they weren't feeling well, or life had handed them lemons, they always found justifications for their own actions. But with others, they didn't extend the same understanding.

Feigning kindness was so easy—pretending to be thoughtful, to be mindful of not burdening others, to care about children and animals. There were no repercussions when they exploited vulnerable, homeless kids by giving them a place to stay and cunningly siphoned off their financial aid. Devoid of guilt, they simply thought they were being clever. They lived off the fat of the land without needing jobs.

Some astute neighbors noticed and pointed fingers. There were also scathing articles aimed at people like them. However, the couple chose to ignore all this, shrugging off the criticisms, because they always had the option to move elsewhere if things got to be too much.

The couple lay in their lavishly decorated bedroom.

"God, it's nice to lie down. The money that came in this time was pretty good. You have to use your head, after all," the husband says.

"You really have no conscience, honey. You don't even feel sorry for the kids, do you?" the wife teased.

"I do feel sorry for them. That's why I got them a set of school supplies—for just ten thousand wons. You know what they say? 'Thank you, sir!'"

The wife guffawed at the husband's words, struggling to catch her breath. "Reputation and conscience don't make for a comfortable bed."

"You are so right."

The couple, so well-matched inside and out, snuggled under their fluffy quilt. They drifted off to sleep and started snoring.

✷ ✷ ✷

In their dream, the couple come across a red truck surrounded by a crowd. There is a tray brimming with free cookies.

Little do they know that their behavior in the dream is not as clever as in reality. The couple are both openly mean and selfish, making no effort to hide their true natures.

As if they had discussed it beforehand, the wife blocks the tray of fortune cookies with her body while the husband jostles through the crowd and begins to scoop up all the free cookies.

Unperturbed by the disappointment of or criticism from others, the couple revel in satisfaction, greedily devouring the cookies as if they were in a competition.

"Ew, what is this?" says the wife. There's a paper note inside the cookie she almost swallowed. She plucks it out of her mouth.

If you sin, not a single night of good sleep awaits you.

"What the heck?" The wife frowns.

"Don't bother. Just throw it away." The husband snatches up the note, crumples it, and throws it on the ground. The golden cookies have a mysterious black-red tint to them, and they're both very sweet and savory. The two amicably pop the rest of the cookies into their mouths.

Soon after consuming the entire batch of fortune cookies, they both drift deeper into sleep.

★ ★ ★

In the next dream, they're being chased by a colossal cat, which looms 100 yards behind them like a tall building. For each desperate stride they make, the cat closes in tenfold. Fiery breath escapes the cat's mouth, scorching the backs of their heads.

The moment they realize the cat resembles the one they abandoned, it transforms into a multitude of children, their towering figures the size of pine trees. Shoulder to shoulder, the children swarm the couple, surrounding them in a gradually tightening circle, ready to flatten them like pancakes.

They begin chanting, "Why did you do it? Did you think no one would know? Why did you do it? Why?!"

The eerie echoes of the hollow-eyed children intensify as the couple gradually sink into the mushy earth, struggling to break free.

This is just a dream. Snap out of it. This can't be real.

They continue to wrestle, straining at the tips of their toes and fingers, desperate to wake up.

Their struggles finally succeed and their eyes flutter open, revealing the familiar sight of their bedroom.

Phew, it really was just a dream. They each let out a sigh of relief, but when they try and turn to face each other, their heads won't move.

"Ugh . . ."

They struggle to speak, their jaw muscles resistant, their lips glued together. They can only manage muffled noises.

Unable to turn their heads, all they can see is the flutter of the bedroom curtains. Did they leave them open? They must have, because they're splitting like the long hair of a *gwisin* in a horror movie, unveiling the monstrous cat that slithers through them from outside. *Arghh!* They try to scream, but no sound escapes. Just then, the cat lunges and pounces on them.

✷ ✷ ✷

"Arghh!"

This time, they each let out a loud yell, jolting awake. Both the husband and wife were drenched in sweat, their hair sticking to their foreheads. They clutched their pounding chests.

Did that come from guilt? they asked themselves. *No. Why would it?*

When they went back to sleep, a similar nightmare replayed. They shuddered. Never had they felt such fear . . . And they didn't know how long the nightmares would continue. Unlike in reality, where they could elude criticism and consequences whenever they wanted, in their dreams they had no freewill. They had been sleeping for only five minutes, but the pain made it feel like an eternity. The couple woke up with blood-shot eyes. It had been the longest, most horrifying night of their lives.

* * *

After that night, nightmares would haunt them every so often, resurfacing just when they believed the horrors were waning. They began to dread going to sleep each night, afraid they'd get trapped inside their dreams again.

Unbeknownst to them, their real-life crimes were about to be exposed to the world, turning reality into a living nightmare. The prospect of a peaceful night's sleep seemed to slip ever further away.

* * *

"So those fortune cookies had Guilt in them? That was why you bought so much Guilt powder back at the Test Center!" Penny says a little too excitedly.

"Hush, Penny. Keep it down," Nicholas urges.

With their stock fully depleted, Penny and Dallergut help Nicholas and Maxim close up the food truck.

"And you didn't eat it because you knew that all along, right, Dallergut?"

"You're right."

"But will that couple be okay? I mean, they cleaned up all the fortune cookies without realizing what they contained. They must be suffering from a lot of Guilt. They could have spared at least one for me. What a bummer. I was curious about the taste—and the message inside . . ."

"If you're curious, I actually have some left from my test batch. You're welcome to have them. But I'd recommend you just take one . . ." Maxim hands Penny a fortune cookie. The shape isn't pretty, but the golden yellow color with the faintest hint of crimson makes it look delicious.

Penny is about to pop it into her mouth when Dallergut stops her. "I suggest you eat it later, after you get home. Even better, hold on to it until you have a relaxing weekend ahead of you. I actually ate a ton of them when Nicholas first started making his test batches."

"And did they make you feel guilty, Dallergut?"

"Well, after I ate them, I called a friend I hadn't talked to in a long time. I had avoided contact for ages with the excuse that I was busy. I guess I *was* subconsciously feeling guilty."

"Did the guilt impact you positively?"

"Surprisingly, yes, it had a very positive effect. More than I expected, in fact. My friend immediately answered the call, and I was so happy to hear his joyful voice. I was nervous I'd get a blunt *What made you call me all of a sudden?* That thought turned out to be outrageous, and he was just as happy to hear from me. We spoke as if no time had passed."

"Ah, Dallergut, maybe you can help promote our fortune cookies," Nicholas says as he closes the truck's side door.

"Nicholas, that's never going to happen. I'm still against giving these fortune cookies to people for free. Why don't you put a more detailed disclaimer on them? Otherwise, you'll have no defense if someone reports you for violating the Information Disclosure Act."

"My goodness, I was wondering when your nagging would start. It's just a delicious cookie with a little bit of guilt mixed in. It's no different from all those sleeping pills and relaxation cookies you give your customers, just with a touch of Guilt. Everyone knows there's no good in eating too much of anything, and it's up to the customer to control themselves. Plus, we're not giving them out to little kids, and the cookies are all legally approved and licensed. Maxim even got a certificate in pastry for it."

"But this is a Guilt cookie, not a Comfort cookie," Penny says as she takes the fortune cookie from Maxim and puts it in her apron pocket.

"What's wrong with guilt? You're not going to tell me it's a useless emotion?"

"Nicholas, all I'm saying is that you should be transparent with your customers about the Guilt. This is not the way to do it." Dallergut remains stern.

"If you market it as a *Guilt-inducing fortune cookie for self-reflection*, you're only going to attract the good people who actually don't need it as much. The people who really need it wouldn't dare come near it."

Penny thinks back to the couple who demolished the entire tray of fortune cookies. If they'd known about the Guilt inside, they wouldn't have been so eager to take them.

"Look at Yasnoozz Otra's dreams. They're not selling, are they? It's just like that."

"They're well-crafted dreams, but if you have an off-putting title like 'Living as a Bully of Mine for a Month,' who's going to buy it? That's just bad marketing."

"I have to disagree. I think Yasnoozz Otra's dreams are spectacular."

"Dallergut, I know you think highly of Otra's dreams, but not everyone is as empathetic as you are," Nicholas says firmly.

Penny turns to Maxim, who is still quietly listening. "Why are you on board with this?" she asks.

"Well, as you know, I debuted with 'Overcoming

Trauma' last year. But as much as I believe that certain difficult memories are worth revisiting, there are other memories that I wish people didn't have to carry in the first place. I believe in the virtue of resilience, but wouldn't it better if there was no need for it? Especially when it's clear who the perpetrators and victims are. I don't want the victims to suffer any more than they already have. I want the hard work of self-reflection to fall to the perpetrators. I want selfish, frivolous, violent people to take this fortune cookie, even if by mistake."

"Maxim, the world doesn't work in black-and-white. An innocent person might end up eating these," says Dallergut, worried.

"Alas, is there anyone completely innocent in this world?" Nicholas chimes in. "Just because we are not behind bars doesn't make us sinless. It's a sin to turn away from the harsh truths of reality. Even I am a sinful old man. Dallergut, just as you love your Calm Cookies, I love my Guilt fortune cookies. I eat them to reflect on how I've lived. Sometimes I feel like I care about kids only once a year as Santa Claus, and pretty much forget them the rest of the year. Christmas is great, but I see more and more kids who suffer so much they don't even get to experience a normal day, let alone a special occasion like Christmas. The older I get, the more I feel this way. I used to think, 'Well, I'm not a hero, I'll just turn a blind eye.' But there's no joy in that life, and it makes me wonder why I've lived like this for so long. I still don't know. But if I continue to remain inside my cabin without making a difference, I probably won't find out until I die . . ." Nicholas pours out his heart as if in penance.

"I feel the same way," Maxim says. "I don't necessarily wish for a world without challenges. What I wish for is the absence of certain evils . . . like atrocities or senseless cruelties that haunt your nights. Like an unshakable lump in your chest. If we could get rid of even just one of these aspects, wouldn't it be as rewarding as saving a life? You see so many people in the news doing bad things and getting away with it. This cookie is for them. I put a warning in the fortune cookies like *If you sin, not a single night of good sleep awaits you*."

Penny has never heard Maxim talk this much the whole time she has known him.

"You know what? Maybe over time that message will become as popular as *If you're not asleep, Santa won't come*," Nicholas says jokingly.

"I hear you, Nicholas. But you should be prepared for some controversy. When you're a celebrity, you're likely to get scrutinized. I don't think you'll fully convince people who have doubts like mine," Dallergut warns.

"I know, and I'll probably go out of business if word spreads, but what if that is exactly part of my grand plan?" Nicholas smiles meaningfully, stroking his snow-white beard.

"Regardless, everything will work out. I have to trust my instincts."

★ ★ ★

The next day, Penny arrives at work early as usual and is reading *Interpretations Better than Dreams*. She is surprised to see an article about Nicholas and Maxim's fortune cookies.

Santa Claus in the Offseason: What's in His Fortune Cookie?

Nicholas, the dreammaker commonly known as Santa Claus, has been traveling around in a red truck lately, handing out cookies. Rumor has it that the cookies contain Guilt, with a cleverly worded message that tricks people into feeling guilty. Whatever his intentions, he is not the saint of justice you see in superhero movies, and is in no position to judge anyone. Who gave him such authority?

Penny suddenly remembers the fortune cookie she left uneaten yesterday. The cookie is soggy after sitting inside her work apron and no longer looks appetizing. She breaks it open and pulls out a small piece of paper.

True happiness is found in a peaceful night's rest, lying
with your legs stretched out and mind at ease.

Between the article and Nicholas's argument, she
can't decide which side she's on. But what she knows
for sure is that the fortune cookie's message is valid.

She plucks up the courage, and bites off half the cookie.
The texture isn't great, but the flavor is okay, sweet and
bitter. Penny waits to see if any guilt creeps in. For a moment, she feels nothing. Then, suddenly, she feels like she
has a heavy pendulum tied around her ankle, like there's
something she should have done that she hasn't.

Then, out of nowhere, two numbers pop into Penny's
head: *330* and *620*. She can't believe she was so focused
on the red truck that she completely forgot about the
two regular customers who have stopped coming in.

Penny is scrambling out of the storage room when
she bumps into Dallergut. He's busy moving a stack of
heavy boxes.

"Dallergut, what brings you to the storage room this
early in the morning?"

"As you can see, I've got some organizing to do," Dallergut says as he dusts off his hands. "You're in early,
Penny."

"Yes, I've also got some work to do this morning.
Oh, by the way, there's something you should know."

"What is it?"

"You may already be aware, but two of our regulars haven't come to the store for a while. They're Customers No. 330 and No. 620—but they haven't filed any complaints."

"I'm glad that you caught on. Good to learn that I'm not the only one who cares about them."

"So you were aware of it. Great. Do you have any ideas for how to bring them back?"

"Well, I don't always have good ideas, but I believe we should kick off with the event."

"You mean that event you were talking about . . . One of your yearly goals?"

"Yes, you remember. We've made significant progress over the past few months. Well, I suppose I can share the details now."

Dallergut carefully opens one of the boxes with his pocketknife, revealing several pillows and duvet covers.

"Are you starting a bedding business or something?"

"Well, that could actually be fun, but I'm going to do something even cooler. I'm going to have a festival that's perfect for our store."

"A festival?"

"Yes. Have you ever been to a pajama party before?"

"You mean where you stay up all night in your paja-mas at a friend's house? Like a sleepover? I had one once when I was very young, and it was a lot of fun. Come to think of it, I don't think I've had one since."

"Get ready. There's going to be a pajama party at our store this fall. No—not just at our store, but in the entire shopping village!"

Penny's eyes widen.

"We're going to have the biggest pajama festival anyone's ever witnessed."

SEVEN
UNSENT INVITATION

It's a relaxing weekend. Only when her back starts to ache does Penny get out of bed and make her way to the living room.

"Oh, you were in your room? I thought you didn't come home last night. I almost went out looking for you," Penny's dad teases as he waters the plants on the balcony.

Penny sprawls out on the couch and uses her toes to press the power button on the television remote control. A burly news anchor is delivering a condensed version of the daily news.

"The leak of Excitement concentrate from an emotion concentrate production plant in the Plant Area has reached the nearby shore, causing high tides along the coast until this evening. If you plan to go to the beach, please be cautious. Next up, an ice-cream truck by Nicholas, the popular dreammaker known as Santa Claus, and Maxim, the young creator of nightmares, has been closed following a controversy. Nicholas acknowledges the issues with the Guilt fortune cookies and has no immediate plans to reopen."

Penny has a sneaking suspicion that Nicholas might have anticipated this, and is already plotting his next move with Maxim in the mountains.

"And for our last news update—a Pajama Festival will be hosted by the Dallergut Dream Department Store in the first week of October. It's reportedly been in the works since the beginning of the year, with careful planning by Mr. Dallergut, sponsoring companies and dreammakers, and workers in the dream industry are on full alert as they follow their progress. Currently, the confirmed sponsors include the bedding company Bedtown Furniture, the National Food Truck Alliance, the Institute for New Technology, and the Nap Research Center. Ingredients from the Test Center of the Company District will be used in large quantities under expert supervision. The festival is scheduled to run around the clock for a week. The streets within a one-mile radius of the Dallergut Department Store are expected to be very crowded, so the committee advises attendees to refrain from wearing shoes and recommends bedroom slippers."

The anchor maintains his usual serious expression, but his voice is filled with excitement.

"Wow! They're finally holding a pajama party! Honey, come over here and look," Penny's dad says, holding a watering can.

"Oh my god, is that true?" Her mom hurries over. She's holding a cleaning brush, which she's been using to scrub the grime off the bathroom tiles. Water drips from her dad's watering can and her mom's cleaning brush. Both are blocking Penny's view.

"Can you please put those down? You guys are making a mess in the living room."

"Penny, did you know that your mom and dad first met at a pajama party?" Mom asks.

"Wait, this isn't Dallergut's first pajama party?"

"No, there was one before. Around twenty-five years ago, wasn't it, honey?"

"Yes, that's right, twenty-five years! About five years after Mr. Dallergut took over the department store. It had a big turnout. Your mom lived in another city back then. She came for the pajama party and met me."

"And we weren't the only couple who met there," Mom adds. "People from all over the world must have come through. There wasn't much to do back then, you know. I fell in love with the city the first time I saw the Dallergut Dream Department Store. There weren't any big dream stores where I lived."

"Wow, that was such a long time ago. How time flies." Dad grins, lost in thought.

"If it did so well back then, why haven't we had another one until now?" Penny asks.

"That's our question to ask you. You work at the store."

"I hadn't heard about it at all until the day before yesterday, and that was by chance. I saw a lot of bedclothes in the storage room. Dallergut said he was going to turn the whole street into a bedroom."

"Yeah? I hope there'll be as many food trucks as there were last time. They gave away expensive emotions in powdered form, sprinkled on various types of desserts. I'll never forget that apple ice cream we ate—it was sprinkled with energizing cinnamon powder. Even back then, your dad would go to sleep by nine o'clock on the dot, but that week, he stayed up two nights in a row, insisting he wasn't tired."

"The first time you two met, you stayed up together for two nights in a row?" Penny asks.

Her parents blush, grab their watering can and cleaning brush, and scurry back to what they were doing.

★ ★ ★

That Monday, the Dallergut Dream Department Store begins the week in mild chaos, with a few confused employees struggling to answer the barrage of questions from customers who have seen the announcement on the news.

"Are you guys really having a pajama party?"

"Oh, yeah. Maybe . . ."

"Will there be new exclusive dreams released at the party?"

"Well, I'm not sure."

"You guys are holding the festival, and you don't know? I just want to know if I need to save my pocket money. Would you please give us some information?"

But the staff really have no idea.

"It would have been nice to have some details, but Dallergut hasn't stepped out of his office today . . ." Penny sulks.

Weather seems unfazed. "I understand why. Our first pajama party was a total flop, and the fallout was too much to handle. Pulling off a big event like that for a single store is a huge task that demands time and effort. We took a hit, so we didn't dare give it another go for a while. I had no clue Dallergut was planning another pajama party, but I get why he'd keep it under wraps until it was certain. Still, it's disappointing to find out through the media instead of hearing it directly from him."

"Wow, I had no idea Dallergut has gone through stuff like that. You two sure share a long history."

"We were both young and passionate back then. Dallergut really wanted to make sure he was taking good care of the dream department store that was passed down from his grandfather, and that passion still drives him."

Right on cue, Dallergut steps out of his office, offering a sheepish smile to his employees as he smooths out his disheveled hair.

"You all must have been dying to see me, I know. I apologize for the confusion. I didn't mean to break the news through the media. I'm sorry. Weather, would you let me use the microphone for a second?"

Dallergut steps toward the front desk, touches the buttons to broadcast throughout the entire floor, and clears his throat.

"Hello, can you hear me okay? To all our employees, please come to the complaint room below my office after lunch break."

The employees assemble in the complaint room after a brisk lunch. They sit in their respective floor groups at a large round table, wearing brooches that show their floor numbers. All the employees are present, except for a few who are needed to keep the store open and operational.

Penny hasn't been in the complaint room since last year when she came down for the group refund case for Maxim's "Overcoming Trauma." Dallergut has set up extra chairs to accommodate everyone, but the round table is a bit too small, causing their legs to touch.

"Hey, Speedo, do you realize your foot is tapping my

shin?" shouts a male employee from the fourth floor, clearly irritated.

"Oh, sorry. I'm getting a little restless sitting around like this. Let's get started, Dallergut," Speedo urges.

"Great, I think we have almost everyone here. I apologize for the delay. I've had to make some last-minute arrangements with the vendors who will provide the necessary supplies for the party. So, the reason I called you all here is to decide on the most important part of the party, the theme." Dallergut looks around the room slowly and adds, "I know we're still missing a few employees here, but let's hear from a veteran staff member from each floor, and then we'll compile our thoughts and make a decision."

Summer from the third floor raises her hand.

"I have a question. Do we need a separate theme? Isn't the idea of lounging in bed in pajamas itself a theme? People should have plenty of fun with it. The store will get more business, too."

"That was exactly how I hosted it last time. I thought it could be that simple, but our first pajama party failed miserably."

Penny also raises her hand and asks, "But my parents remember it very fondly. What makes you think it was a failure?"

"That's a great question, Penny," Dallergut says. "There

are very clear criteria. We spent a lot of money, but our revenue didn't improve at all. Our goal for the party was to bring back the regular customers who stopped coming, but none of them returned. All we got was a temporary boost in foot traffic that didn't last. So, this time, I thought we could have a specific theme and exclusive dreams related to the theme."

"So the dreams need to be accessible enough for returning customers who might be coming back for the first time after years, right?" Weather cuts to the chase.

"Exactly, Weather. I would need recommendations for dreams everyone can enjoy, whether they be newcomers or regulars or those returning customers whom we want to lure back after a long absence."

"Well, if you're looking for something accessible for the returning customers, how about our second floor's dreams? 'Daily' dreams are timeless and familiar to all of us . . ."

As soon as the employees on the second-floor start talking, the employees on the other floors look bored, especially Motail from the fifth floor. "But it's still a pajama party after all," he says. "Wouldn't it be nice to have some fun and fantastical dreams?"

"What dreams would the fifth floor like to offer? You sound like you have good alternatives," snaps Vigo Myers, the second-floor manager.

"Oh, you've got to be kidding. We're the discount floor. Our dreams should be out of the question."

"Well, the third-floor dreams certainly go with the festivities," Mogberry says confidently.

"Yes. What could be more fitting for the party than cinematic dreams and flying dreams? I actually think it's a waste of time even to discuss this." Summer echoes Mogberry's sentiment.

Speedo immediately throws cold water on her idea. "If you put it that way, wouldn't the bestsellers on the first floor be more suitable? We can't just have our fourth-floor nap dreams at the party, so I'd rather go with the first-floor dreams."

"Speedo, I don't think first-floor dreams are a realistic option. These all-time award-winning dreams or best-selling dreams would run out quickly because there aren't enough of them coming in." Weather shakes her head and looks over at Penny, who is sitting next to her. "Penny, what do you think?"

Penny looks at a palm-sized note she pulled from her apron pocket. She tries to reference some of her notes from reading *Interpretations Better than Dreams*.

"Since this is a festival, some people might be buying dreams as gifts. In that light, I'd say the dynamic dreams on the third floor would be best . . ." Penny looks at her scribbled note:

What makes a good dream?

1. a captivating, timeless storyline, like a movie you want to watch over and over
2. a dream customized for each individual dreamer
3. fantastical experiences that are only possible in dreams

"Which dreams have timeless allure, feel bespoke and offer content unique to the dream realm?" she says.

"Does such a dream even exist that meets all these criteria?" The staff exchange murmurs and glances.

"Yes. On the second floor." Vigo Myers breaks the silence, confidently raising his hand. "Our dreams in the Memories corner check all these boxes. Memories are meant to be revisited over time, and since everyone's memories are different, they're naturally customized. And where else can you experience past memories but in a dream?"

"You have a point." Dallergut nods.

"Then, how about *Memories* for the theme? I could ask some dreammakers I work with to make dreams about memories. That way, it doesn't have to be limited to dreams already stocked on the third floor," Mogberry suggests.

The others begin to agree, one by one, until most of the staff are in favor.

"All right, team. We now have the theme for the festival. *Memories*," Dallergut announces. "It's time to show-case your talents. We don't have much time, and every minute counts from now on. If this goes well, it will become an annual event for our city, the kind everyone looks forward to. Picture the main street adorned with all sorts of fluffy, feel-good decorations all around our dream shops! Imagine food trucks from all over the country, with people strolling in their newly purchased pajamas for a night out at our festival." Dallergut is standing now, his arms spread wide.

Now that the theme is fixed, discussions ramp up. Employees start dividing up the tasks.

"We'll need data on each and every one of our customers," Motail says.

"But who's going to organize all that paperwork?" asks Penny.

"I bet it's already organized," Motail says, as he looks at the determined staff from the second floor, already discussing plans under Vigo Myers's direction.

"I've been analyzing our customers' tastes based on their dream purchases. It's a hobby of mine," one of the second-floor staff members says.

"Amazing. We're in such good hands." Myers seems content.

"I've even organized them by month, like which wrapping paper colors sell the most in the fall. Do you want to take a look?"

The second-floor staff's commitment to tidiness sur-passes Penny's expectations.

"When are you going to go through all that? It'll take me forever to come up with a dream list," Penny mutters to herself.

"For me, half a day should do. Man, it's been a while. I'm so ready to flex some muscles." Speedo anticipates the task like a hyena eyeing its prey, cracking his knuck-les before digging into the second-floor staff's massive pile of data files.

"Hold up, everyone." Weather raises her hand to draw their attention. "Mind if I take over the party decora-tions?"

"Of course. That was going to be my biggest head-ache," someone says. The others agree.

"Oh my god. I'm so excited! I can decorate the entire storefront and the alleyways just the way I want! I'm go-ing to make it unforgettable and fill the whole city with fluffy things."

"Yes, Weather—and don't you worry about the budget," Dallergut says, holding out a thick envelope. Weather's eyes widen, and an excited grin spreads across her face as she grabs the envelope. "I need to get started—right now! You said you've got all the bedding for the party? I'll take care of the smaller items."

★ ★ ★

The party preparations go smoothly, with each person doing what they do best. Weather sketches out what she envisions for the party's aesthetic. Penny is amazed at her drawing skills.

Speedo moves through the next steps faster than anyone else, creating a perfect dream list with the theme of memories. Social butterfly Mogberry leverages her extensive connections to recruit up-and-coming dreammakers, while Vigo Myers meticulously sifts through the test dreams, which arrive one after another.

As the news spreads, everyone seems to be talking about the upcoming pajama party. Customers are equally excited. Middle-aged and older customers, including Penny's parents, fondly reminisce about the first pajama party from years past.

"Ah, the good old days. I can't wait to stay up all night again before I get too old. I'll make sure to take my nutritional supplements before the festival."

"This time, we've got Bedtown Furniture and the National Food Truck Alliance attached, and we're going to have new product presentations from up-and-coming dreammakers! Just imagine—it's going to be so much fun. This will be my first full-on pajama party. I'm so excited!" Mogberry, bursting with excitement, roams around each floor, engaging in lively chitchat with customers.

As the list of sponsoring companies expands, anticipation grows, and word spreads that multiple dreammakers will showcase their memories-themed dreams.

"My kids are already pestering me to get new pajamas," Weather says.

"I've also been eyeing new sleepwear. I'm thinking of bringing it to work, so I can change and head straight out to the party afterward. How does that sound? No one will be able to tell who's from here and who's from out of town." Penny is equally excited. "I heard that the New Technology Lab will showcase a bunch of new tech products, like an expo. Maybe we can try out the 'Dream for Two' and dream the same dream simultaneously."

"I'm sorry, but that's still in development. I doubt it'll ever be complete in my lifetime," Weather says with a hint of resignation.

It seems they can easily spend a whole day just talking about the pajama party.

"Excuse me, I have a package for Mrs. Weather. Is she here?" A deliveryman stands in the doorway, holding a large box.

"Oh my! That came quicker than expected." Weather jumps to her feet.

"Yep. Our boss prioritized your order and printed them first. I know everyone's looking forward to the pajama party. Please write your name here and sign."

"Please pass on my sincere thanks!" Weather signs the form. She swiftly tears open the box, displaying a practiced ease. She must have opened thousands of them.

"What's all this?" Penny asks.

"Our party invitations. A must-have for any event!"

THE DALLERGUT DREAM DEPARTMENT STORE
INVITES YOU TO THE PAJAMA FESTIVAL

**IN THE FIRST WEEK OF OCTOBER,
WHEN THE GENTLE FALL AIR SETTLES IN,
WE'RE EXCITED TO INVITE YOU TO A WEEK-LONG,
DAY-AND-NIGHT CELEBRATION.
THE THEME OF THE PARTY IS MEMORIES.
COME AND ENJOY ALL OUR MEMORY-THEMED DREAMS,
WITH PLENTY TO SEE, DO AND EAT!
WE LOOK FORWARD TO SEEING YOU IN YOUR SLEEP,
JUST AS WE ALWAYS DO.**

—FROM ALL OF US AT THE DALLERGUT DREAM DEPARTMENT STORE—

"I made a special invite for our regulars. If we start mailing it out today, all our regulars should receive it within a week."

"But will they remember getting an invitation?"

"If they don't remember it when they're awake, I'm sure they will when they're here while they're asleep.

The fun of the party starts with sending out the invitations, so my party's just begun," Weather says cheerfully.

"Ahem." Vigo Myers coughs awkwardly as he approaches the front desk.

"Hello, Myers. Do you need anything?" Penny asks.

Myers keeps glancing up at the front desk. "Actually, yes. Can I take one of them?" He points to the stack of invitations with the tip of his chin.

"Of course! Please!" Penny nods vigorously. She has a feeling she knows who Myers wants to invite.

That afternoon, Customer No. 1 visits the store, and as expected, Myers approaches her. He has been lingering around the lobby with the invitation in his hands. With strides as awkward as those of a tin robot, he walks up to her.

"Excuse me, miss."

"Yes?"

"We're having a party this fall and would like you to attend. Here's an invitation."

"Wow, what kind of party is it?"

"It's a pajama party. You'll love it. I would like for you to come."

As the customer reads it through, Myers stands there without a word, anxiously waiting for her response. She nods with a smile and is about to pass him by when he stammers nervously.

"Wait—actually . . . You won't remember this, but this is not my first invitation to you. I was clumsy back then. But this time, you can come as you are. You don't have to change into outerwear before going to bed . . . or hide from others. I've been meaning to invite you like this, but you can just go to sleep in your regular pajamas."

"I'm sorry, but isn't that an obvious choice of clothes?" she asks, perplexed.

Myers runs upstairs, leaving her there, dumbfounded. Penny thinks she catches a glimpse of him looking somewhat relieved.

A short while later, Mogberry comes to the front desk with Summer from the third floor.

"Hey, Weather, I have an idea for the party. How about we set up a mat and offer a free *The Time God and the Three Disciples* personality test inside the department store? It would give customers something more to enjoy when they come in. What do you think? This could be a huge hit!" Mogberry exclaims.

"I was telling her that personality tests are out of style. They were only trendy several months ago," Summer interjects.

"Well, I think it's a good idea," Weather replies.

"See? I told you! We should do this together, Summer. You're in this with me, okay?" says Mogberry, linking arms with Summer. Summer shoots Weather a resentful look as Mogberry drags her away from the front desk.

"The whole staff seems pumped up for the party."

"Couldn't agree more. Penny, I'll leave the invitations here, so make sure to hand them out to our regulars when they come to the store, even when I'm not here. Okay?"

***

Over the next few days, Penny passes out invitations to almost all the regulars. There are two invitations left—for Customers No. 330 and 620.

"I can't give out invitations if they don't come."

"There's still time. We'll just have to wait and see," Weather says.

"I wonder why they don't come anymore?"

"You've been very intrigued by this lately, Penny."

"I just wish there was more I could do."

"What sparked this interest?"

"Well . . . I'm not exactly sure, but I think it started with my visit to the Civil Complaint Center. Meeting with Customer No. 792 and Customer No. 1 got me thinking a lot."

"If that's the reason, then Dallergut's policy of taking second-year employees to the Civil Complaint Center seems to be working very well," Weather remarks, giving Penny a satisfied look.

"Yeah, or maybe it's the personality test. You know, the one Mogberry was talking about. I took it earlier this year."

"I took it, too, and came out as a *Third Disciple* type. I believe it was a wise mediator or something. How about you, Penny?"

"I came out as a *Second Disciple* type. Do you happen to know who the descendants of the Second Disciple are? No one seems to know."

"Well, I can understand why. It's because he isn't around here much. He likes to keep a low profile."

"I'm sure I've heard the name, though . . ."

"Atlas," says Weather.

Penny finally remembers where she heard the name. First, she heard it mentioned by Myers, and then again in the conversation between Nicholas and Maxim in front of a sack of Emotion Powder at the Test Center.

"Where is he, and what's he up to? I've heard people talking about him, but I've never seen him myself."

"Atlas is . . ." Weather begins to say something, but Dallergut bursts out of his office. He's dressed in his off-site business shoes with a thin robe slung over his arm.

"Where are you heading, Dallergut?"

"I have a quick trip to make. And I need to take the invitations with me. I see there are two left, as expected."

"Where are you taking them? Are you going to the Civil Complaint Center?"

"I've identified where these two customers are. And fortunately, they're a little closer than the complaint center."

"Where is that?"

"Penny was just asking about Atlas, Dallergut," Weather chimes in.

"Was she? Well, then. Care to join me, Penny?"

Penny's confused. What do the missing customers, the invitations and Atlas have to do with each other?

"Where are we going?"

"You'll know when we get there. Come on, hurry up. We have to catch the commuter train."

"You're taking the train at this hour?" Penny asks, her short hair bouncing lightly as she tilts her head.

* * *

A moment later, Penny finds herself on the train with Dallergut. The late summer air is sticky, but when the train picks up speed, a cool breeze accompanies it, making the ride much more comfortable. After a few minutes of silence, Dallergut finally speaks up.

"Penny, you must not tell anyone what you're about to see and hear tonight. Not that I expect you to."

"What's that? Aren't we just going to find the two customers?"

"You'll find out when we get there. I don't want people to know where we're going. It would be nice if we could keep the place as quiet and exclusive as it is."

"Again, I don't know where this place is . . ."

"We're already here. Let's get off."

The train comes to a stop, and Dallergut gets up.

They are at the lowest point of the Dizzying Downhill, the location of the concession stand and the Noctiluca Laundry.

Still puzzled, Penny follows Dallergut, who is clearly heading toward the Noctiluca Laundry.

"Dallergut, aren't we going to find the customers? Why the laundry?"

Instead of answering the question, Dallergut greets a Noctiluca at the entrance.

"You're finally here! We've been waiting for you. And I see that you have company!" The Noctiluca, whose tail has just a little blue fur at the tip, grins at Penny. It is none other than Assam.

"Assam! You really did start working in the laundry! Now, can anyone fill me in as to why we're here?"

"You'll find out when you get in," Assam replies. He's behaving in just the same mysterious way as Dallergut. Penny feels her patience wearing thin.

Assam points to the back of the cave, urging Penny on while Dallergut marches right in. Assam's large build and Dallergut's tall body block half the entrance. Penny stands behind them, peering suspiciously into the darkness of the cave, the wooden sign that reads *Noctiluca Laundry* rattling precariously in the wind.

"This is no ordinary laundry, is it?"

Penny hears a faint sound of rippling water from inside the cave. A cool breeze drifts out, an irresistible lure on a clammy day like today. The dark laundry beckons her forward.

Struggling to connect the dots between Atlas, the descendant of the Second Disciple, the two invitations she has yet to deliver, and the laundry, Penny follows Assam and Dallergut into the cave.

EIGHT

THE NOCTILUCA LAUNDRY

Penny, Dallergut and Assam move deeper into the cavern. The spacious passageway allows the Noctilucas to carry large loads of laundry with ease. Only a few steps in, the cave becomes pitch-dark. But Assam's blue tail shines like a glow-in-the-dark star leading the way. Penny and Dallergut tread cautiously, watching out for Assam's tail.

The distant gurgle of water continues.

"This feels like walking through an underground drainage ditch beneath a mountain," says Penny nervously from behind Dallergut.

As they continue walking, keeping pace with Assam's pattering footsteps, a sudden flash of light bathes the passage. The walls are rugged and uneven, but the ruggedness seems to be intentional. Faint light seeps through the cracks.

Just then, a rippling shadow makes the wall go dark. It isn't Assam's shadow or Dallergut's or Penny's. Yet there are no other objects in the passage that could have cast it. The shadow seems to hesitate for a moment before converging with others moving across the ceiling.

"Whoa! Dallergut, Assam, did you just see that? The shadows are moving on their own, shifting and twisting! And they are definitely not ours." Penny lets out a startled yell, and Assam spins around. He brings his front paw to his mouth. "Shhh! You have to keep quiet in here. Okay?"

"Please understand, Assam. It can be surprising for someone who's never seen anything like this before," Dallergut says, and Assam nods kindly.

The deeper they get inside the cave, the more the shimmering shadows make it feel like they're underwater. Monotonous music lingers in the air, continuously drifting in and out. As they become accustomed to the sound, their surroundings grow brighter. Penny can now make out the shapes of the Noctilucas working in the open space at the end of the passage.

"Phew, what a relief to see some light. Hey, Assam, why do we have to be so quiet in here? And what were those shadows?"

"Because this is not just a laundry, it's also a place where people and shadows stop to rest," Assam replies, looking back at Penny.

"They rest in the laundry?"

As Penny ponders this, Dallergut, who has been walking ahead, stops in his tracks and points to one side of the cave. A familiar phrase is carved into the wall.

THE SECOND DISCIPLE AND THEIR FOLLOWERS WERE TRAPPED IN ONLY THE GOOD MEMORIES, SO THEY COULD NOT ACCEPT THE PASSAGE OF TIME, THE INEVITABLE PARTINGS AND DEATHS. THE TEARS OF THEIR SOULS CONSTANTLY FLOWED DOWN TO THE EARTH, CREATING A LARGE CAVE.

Dallergut reads the passage in a low voice. It is about the Second Disciple from the tale of *The Time God and the Three Disciples*.

"Why is that inscription carved here? Could this be . . . the cave in the story where the Second Disciple and their followers are said to have gone into hiding?"

"Indeed, this is the cave of Atlas, a descendant of the Second Disciple. The Time God granted his ancestors the ability to remember many things for a long time, and this cave is a testament to that power. It's a collection of unforgettable events from the past, as you see here. We call them *memories*."

Dallergut gestures with his hand, tracing the perimeter of the wall around the inscription. Adorning the cave walls are sparkling gemstones, their size ranging from as small as a bead to something much larger than a thumbnail. They emit a warm glow.

"All these sparkling crystals are actually people's memories. Unbelievable, isn't it? It may sound hyperbolic to say this cave was built from the tears of the descendants of the Second Disciple, but it's true that they made this place their home and stayed here for a very long time. But even they didn't spend their entire lives here. Except Atlas. He was different. He has dedicated his entire life to this cave—even to this day," Dallergut explains in a calm, low voice. Penny can barely believe her eyes.

"Penny, you see some of the crystals are more firmly embedded inside the walls? These are strong memories. They have the power to uphold other memories. That's why this cave is stronger than any other kind of structure," Assam says proudly.

The entire cave looks like the night sky, with the strong memories embedded in it like constellations of stars. Penny can't take her eyes off the memory crystals as she moves deeper in.

"Assam, why does this place pretend to be a laundry?"

"What're you talking about? It's not a pretense. It *is* a laundry."

"It is? But you said this is where people and shadows stop to rest. Is it a shelter, or a laundry, or Atlas's cave . . . ? What is this place exactly?"

"Patience, kid. You'll find out soon. Now, come on in. Welcome to my new workplace!"

* * *

At the end of the passageway, the group steps into an unexpectedly spacious area, and Penny wonders how such a large space could be hidden away, out of sight. Large washing machines are neatly stacked under a ceiling so high it dwarfs even the Noctilucas, who bustle about, surrounded by laundry baskets hastily woven from soft branches. On one side, rows of tall poles serve as sturdy supports for clotheslines, heavy with dry sleepwear.

The repetitive noise of the washing machines, the rhythmic splashing of water against fabric, creates a melodic ambience.

Unlike Assam, the majority of the Noctilucas are a vibrant blue all over. Carrying laundry baskets using their front paws and tails, they skillfully navigate through the space. Their luminous blue fur casts a radiant glow throughout the cave. It triggers memories of the glow-in-the-dark stickers Penny used to stick to her ceiling and stare at as a child.

"Everyone, look. Assam has brought guests," the bluest Noctiluca exclaims, calling for attention.

"Ahhh, my back hurts. I was actually waiting for you."

The sound comes from a small figure, concealed in the shadows amid the Noctilucas, swiftly gathering fallen laundry and putting it back into the basket as though harvesting ears of barley. Straightening his back, he looks rugged and suntanned like a farmer.

"Dallergut, this new staff member must be reliable if you've brought them all the way here," the man remarks. Stepping forward, he brushes past Dallergut to shake Penny's hand, catching her off guard with the rough calluses on his palm. Dallergut meets him with a smile.

"Welcome. You must be Penny," the man greets her. "I heard about you from Dallergut and Assam. And someone else too . . . Never mind, I'd better not tell you that." He fumbles. "This is the cave of the Second Disciple, who has the ability to remember everything for a long time. We've been guarding this space carved with people's memories for generations."

"Excuse me, but you are . . . ?" Penny feels that she already knows the answer.

"Atlas. A descendant of the Second Disciple. I'm sure you're wondering why this place became a laundry." He seems to have read Penny's mind.

"Penny, let me show you something even more unbelievable." Assam picks up a soaking nightgown and lays it over the clothesline closest to the memory crystals. The light from the memories seeps into the fabric, miraculously turning the material fluffy and dry. Penny watches the magic unfold in awe.

"The light of memories can dry wet clothes beautifully, as if they hadn't been wet in the first place. The descendants of the Second Disciple discovered this long ago. They offered the Noctilucas a collaboration, and the Noctilucas had no reason to refuse. They already had enough trouble washing and drying hundreds of sets of pajamas a day. Since then, this has become our invaluable workplace," Assam explains to Penny with pride.

"I see—well, sort of. But, hey, Dallergut, you haven't forgotten what we're here for, right? To find our regular customers and hand out the invitations. Are you sure they're here?" Penny asks, keeping their mission in mind.

"They are definitely here, Penny. Am I right, Atlas?" Dallergut asks, and Atlas gestures toward an area strewn with massive piles of sleepwear.

"Well, of course. The two customers you talked about are both here. Go ahead and meet them."

"That's great. Follow me, Penny."

Penny follows Dallergut, brushing aside the cluttered laundry as they move farther into the cave.

★ ★ ★

Penny spots a hidden alcove behind the piles of laundry. Instead of clotheslines, people in pajamas rest on hammocks suspended between wooden poles. Amid the heap of unwashed laundry, an older woman sits alone, listening to the clanking and whirring of the washing machines. Even from a distance, Penny recognizes her face at once.

"I remember her! She used to come to the store every morning and take her time browsing the catalog. She must be Customer No. 330! We've found one of two."

Penny starts toward her excitedly, but Dallergut grabs her by the collar.

"Penny, before you go and talk to her, I need you to know why she's here. You just heard the story earlier about how this place started using the light of memories to dry the laundry, right?"

"Yes."

"There's more to the story. Atlas found out that not only does this light help dry damp laundry, but it also has a soothing effect on people's minds. Memories possess the power to ease the hearts of those who find themselves submerged in lethargy."

"Lethargy?"

"Yes. At times, when people don't feel like doing anything, they shut their eyes and sleep, even if they're not sleepy. In that kind of sleep, they're not looking for dreams, they just want to shut themselves off from the world completely. They aimlessly stroll down the street or linger in front of any store they come across, not just ours, without entering. Now, does that give you an idea of who brought them here?"

"Someone who spots them wandering aimlessly down the street and brings them here . . . It has to be a Noctiluca!"

"You're right on," Dallergut confirms, satisfied with Penny's answer. "The older Noctilucas with blue fur— they've been observing the out-of-town customers for a long time, so they have a knack for recognizing customers who are lethargic and don't want to do anything."

"I see. If that's the case, Dallergut, it might be rude of me to force the invitation on Customer No. 330. What if she's not interested in attending?"

"Well, I don't think so. Lethargy happens to everyone. I know it happens to me. In times like these, shouldn't we be the ones to extend a hand? She is one of our regulars, after all."

Dallergut carefully approaches the customer. She gives him a sideways glance, closes her eyes, and refocuses on the sound of the washing machines.

Dallergut initiates the conversation. "Isn't it so peaceful? I find the sound of washing machines calming."

"Yeah . . . Can I help you?"

"Well, to get to the point, we're having a big festival at our dream department store with the theme of memories. We'd love to invite you and share some amazing dreams."

"I'm not interested. I don't want to do anything, so if you'd just leave me alone."

"I see. We all feel that way sometimes. When you think about it, though, aren't we a lot like those pajamas in the washing machines?" Dallergut asks.

The customer stares at Dallergut's face, as if asking *What the hell are you talking about?*

"Laundry gets soaked one minute and dries the next. We all get soaked in all sorts of emotions, don't we? And then, it's back to normal, like any other day. So, how about we dry them off?"

"How?" She looks a bit intrigued, and Dallergut, not missing the moment, holds out the invitation.

"All you need is a little nudge. You know how sometimes, the smallest of actions can make you feel better, like talking on the phone with a friend or going for a quick stroll? This time, allow us to give you a nudge with the promise of dreams based on the theme of memories. We will help you feel better. Would you be willing to try and come to the Pajama Festival?"

Regular No. 330 of the Dallergut Dream Department Store was a woman in her midsixties.

A decade ago, she had gracefully navigated meno-pause and was now enjoying her retirement after a long and successful career. She and her husband had raised three children, who had all left to start their own fami-lies. When the youngest had got married, she'd returned from the wedding and was winding down, thinking she had now fulfilled all the major roles in her life—and an unexpected lethargy overtook her.

In hindsight, her days had become a string of mun-dane routines that nobody else seemed to acknowledge. The realization that her thirty-five-year career had come to an end, coupled with an empty nest and a silent house, struck her chest like a hard rubber ball. Her friends and family told her that all she needed to do now was rest. But their words didn't sit well with her. In fact, they sounded unpleasant.

Suddenly, the woman was an age at which she had to consider herself fortunate that her health was holding up well. As she washed her face and gazed into the mirror, an awkwardness crept in, as if reuniting with a long-lost friend after the whirlwind of raising kids and working. She swapped the large mirror for a smaller one. But as she studied her husband's aging face beside hers, the un-deniable traces of time that had woven through both of them could not be overlooked.

Eventually, little routines like brewing morning tea or

taking out the trash became challenging for her. Sometimes, she would try to mix up her routine by cooking new side dishes or growing different vegetables in her garden, but she could never escape the overwhelming sense of lethargy that was slowly consuming her.

What was my life for . . . ?

Up until then, she'd had all these target milestones that had kept her going—paying off the mortgage, sending all her kids to college, and seeing them all happily married. Now that this was all done, she'd lost her sense of purpose and started to miss having those goals.

The woman no longer had anything to live for or to look forward to. Unable to overcome her lethargy, she forced herself to sleep even when she didn't need it.

In her dream, she wanders aimlessly like a lost person.

"Are you lost, not knowing where to go? Or have you lost your will to do anything?" asks a nearby Noctiluca, as if reading her mind. He is covered in blue fur from head to toe. "Would you care to join me? I know the perfect resting place for someone in your predicament."

As soon as the woman nods, the Noctiluca gently lifts her onto his tail. When she loses her balance, he wraps it around her more tightly, giving her the support she needs.

The Noctiluca takes her to the commuter train and covers her with a pile of laundry. Surprisingly, the laundry is clean, with a cozy cotton smell. She can rest undisturbed underneath.

That's how she ends up following the Noctiluca into the laundry.

★ ★ ★

Dallergut and Penny, having safely delivered the invitation to Customer No. 330, are now making their way to the farthest corner of the laundry to locate Customer No. 620—the last remaining regular. In a room with a slightly lowered ceiling, large couches await them. Memory crystals are embedded in the cave walls, emitting enough of a glow to illuminate the space. Three Noctilucas are sitting around folding dry laundry, their jokes and giggles echoing off the cave walls.

"There's 620," whispers Dallergut.

"What? Where?"

Penny takes a few more steps and spots a man among the Noctilucas. He is diligently folding sleeping socks.

Penny initiates the conversation this time. "Hello, Customer No. 620."

"Me?" replies the man. He looks to be in his mid-twenties.

"Yes. Would you mind sparing some time for us?

Looks like you deserve some rest." Penny gestures toward a neat pile of dry laundry.

"At least it gives me something to do. It helps me to feel alive. I know I can't accomplish anything big, but I want to keep myself busy."

"May I ask how you're doing?" Penny asks as she gently sits next to him.

"Nothing much to say. I'm just . . . very tired."

He was well regarded as a hardworking young man. His friends thought he was living his days to their fullest, and his juniors looked up to him as a role model. He believed that constant movement was the only way to keep his mind from wandering, and in many cases, he seemed right. He didn't understand why people wallowed in meaningless depression or how anyone could get so caught up in their emotions that they failed to do what needed to be done.

His driving force was always his family. As he reached the age of independence, his sole ambition was to achieve success swiftly for their sake. He dreamed of gifting his dad a new car, freeing him from the constant cycle of repairs on his aged vehicle. He dreamed of opening a credit card with a generous limit for his mom. Only that moment never seemed to come. Occasionally, he couldn't help but reflect on how old he and his parents would be by the time he finally achieved the stability he aimed for.

Luck never seemed to be on the man's side. It became evident that sheer hard work couldn't tip the scales in his favor, whether it came to passing an exam or securing a coveted job with a perpetually long waiting list.

For every opportunity he let slip away, his future plans were being pushed back further and further.

Your current experiences will help you in the long run, one way or another. You can never face too many challenges in your youth. They are the cornerstones of the most brilliant successes.

The man had once saved these words as his smart-phone background, as an encouraging reminder. But now, he had deleted them. The phrase seemed like something that only someone who was doing well could say.

The man's motivation dwindled.

He craved a mental reset, and the easiest way to take care of himself was to lie down with his eyes closed. He felt certain that parts of him were malfunctioning.

I wish I could be rebooted like a computer so all my glitches would be gone in one fell swoop, he mused.

Robotically, he fell asleep and woke up. Falling asleep was easy, but getting back up required determination. The lethargy was beyond his control. The man dared not utter the word *depression*, fearing it would consume him entirely. Consequently, no one was aware of his condition. As much as he wanted to get out of his dreams and get on with his life, his body was a limp noodle. He repeatedly attempted to drift off to sleep, flicking off the lights in his room, regardless of the hour. The time he spent lying down grew longer and longer.

✷ ✷ ✷

Customer No. 620 calmly recounts his story and graciously accepts the invitation. The whole time, his hands remain in motion, helping the Noctilucas fold the sleeping socks.

"I heard simple, repetitive work helps you pull yourself together," the man remarks, attempting to sound cheerful. Penny can't help but feel a pang of compassion for him.

"I completely agree," Assam chimes in. "I used to do my laundry here as well. The act of hanging and folding the laundry was incredibly soothing. I couldn't wait to get older so I could work here." He's scanning the man's surroundings, holding an unlit flashlight.

"Whoa, Assam, you surprised me. What are you looking for, popping out of nowhere like that?" Penny can't understand what he's doing. But just then, the space beneath the man's feet starts to darken.

"Look at this!" the man exclaims. "There's something strange under my feet . . ."

The dark shadow shifts and takes on the shape of a human. It grows larger and larger until it completely surrounds the man. Penny gasps as the shadow almost swallows him up.

"Hey, get away!" Assam shines his flashlight at the shadow. His sudden shout startles Dallergut, causing him to knock over a pile of sleeping socks. The dark shadow, suddenly bathed in light, shrinks and transforms into the shape of a baby cradled in the man's arms.

"I know you guys love people," Assam warns the shadow, "but you shouldn't bother your master."

With that, it shrinks even further, circling at the man's feet.

"What is this, Assam?" Penny asks on behalf of the man, who looks as confused as she feels.

"This is the customer's night shadow. Because its master has locked himself into this laundry without dreaming, it tracked him and found its way here. They're not bad guys, but they're clingy, and if you can't shake them off, you won't wake up refreshed. That's the thing, Customer 620," Assam grumbles, "when it sticks on you, all this time you spend resting is a complete waste." The shadow at the man's feet slithers off the wall and into the darkness, sullen.

"Still, it's a lot easier to catch a shadow than it is to chase down and dress a naked customer. I'm glad I'm old enough to work here now instead." Penny's happy to hear how content Assam is working at the laundry.

"I also like this place," Penny agrees. "If only more people knew about it so they could rest here. Don't you think so, Dallergut?"

"Actually, there's no profit to be made here," Dallergut responds, calmly shaking his head. "Nobody in the industry would want customers to hide out here and not buy dreams. Besides, people might take issue with the fact that we're just sheltering people who won't dream, instead of tackling the actual problem."

"Like . . . people from the Civil Complaint Center?"

"Could be. That's their job, after all. We can't survive without selling dreams, so they might try to shut this place down or force us to start selling dreams here. Few people realize that sometimes it is best to wait," Dallergut says bitterly. "So it's for the best that this place is only known to those who truly need it. At least, that's what Atlas thinks. And we can't let people stay here too long. It's not a place to stay forever. Everyone needs shelter, but wouldn't it be a shame if you became too comfortable here and never returned to where you came from?"

Meanwhile, the night shadows are lurking around them again.

Those who can't shake off their cuddly shadows wear a puzzled look, like the frown you get when you're struggling to get out of bed in the morning.

"If you don't let go of your master right away, you won't be able to make any more of your favorite memories," Dallergut warns, and the shadows scatter away as if they understand him.

"I think I'll head back. Penny, are you done here?" Assam asks.

"Yeah."

"Then, we can go out together. Mr. Dallergut, shall we get going?" Assam asks, but Dallergut seems preoccupied with the other customers in the cave. Assam adds, "They should be fine. Atlas is always here so they won't be alone. Plus, the other Noctilucas will arrive at dawn."

"Of course. I guess my work here for the day is done. Let's say goodbye to Atlas and get back to work."

✱ ✱ ✱

When they head back to the laundry entrance, they see Noctilucas shuffling out of the cave in single file. All the washing machines except for a few have stopped.

"Looks like we're not the only guests here," Dallergut says, pointing toward Atlas's cave house.

Penny spots two captivating figures. One looks out

of place in a desaturated blue *dopo* robe, the waist se-
cured with a thin tulle sash, his hair tied in a knot. The
other, a tall woman, wears a sleek, formfitting suit. She
has short hair. Penny recalls the newspaper article about
Doje, the elusive, seldom-seen creator behind "Meeting
with the Dead" dreams. She can hardly believe her eyes.
He's standing before her now, accompanied by Yasnoozz
Otra.

The two are deep in conversation with Atlas when they
both pivot to gaze at Dallergut and Penny. For the first
time, Penny can see Doje up close. His penetrating eyes
and otherworldly presence contrast sharply with Otra's
immaculate modern style, as if one of them is from the
past and the other from the present, each having emerged
from a time machine that just so happens to resemble a
washing machine.

Doje stares into Penny's face, sending a chill down her
spine and causing her body to stiffen. Perhaps her fear
stems from the kind of dreams he creates.

Fortunately, Otra recognizes Penny and breaks the silence. "Penny, is that you?"

Penny fumbles for a response. "Hey . . . Um . . . Are
you two coming to the Pajama Festival?"

"Ah, I heard about that! I know several dreammakers
are working on dreams around the theme of memories.
I'm sure the party will be a great opportunity for them.

Dallergut, may Doje and I join as well?" asks Otra enthusiastically, rolling up the sleeves of her thin blouse.

"Of course. The whole experience will definitely be better with your help."

"The theme is memories this time?" Atlas chimes in. "I'm sure our ancestors would be deeply touched to hear that. We descendants hold memories very dearly. Memories have a way of growing stronger the more we recall them. By the time the festivities are over, this cave will shine even brighter. And the laundry will dry better, of course." He grins.

"Honorable Dallergut, might I seek your gracious consent to create a lantern from the memory crystals?" These are the first words Doje speaks to them, and Penny notes the distinct, old-fashioned charm of his speech. "It would be a splendid idea to gather memory crystals from the departed and fashion a lantern with them," he continues. "I believe it would beautifully complement the Pajama Festival's theme. What say you?"

"A lantern made of the memories of the departed . . . I'm afraid it will remind the outsiders of the idiom *their life flashed before their eyes*." Dallergut seems unsettled.

"Can you enlighten me as to what you mean?" Doje asks.

"The lanterns are a fitting idea, but I don't think they're appropriate for the festivities . . . What if you create a dream that captures the memories of the dead?" Dallergut offers as a counterproposal.

"By the way, I bet the theme had something to do with Vigo Myers, the second-floor manager, didn't it? His stubbornness is second to none," Otra says.

"Well, he sure wanted the theme, but it was Penny here who cleverly steered the decision," Dallergut says.

"I see! No wonder Maxim likes you, Penny. Oops, I'm so sorry. I can't help but meddle in young people's business."

Penny blinks, unsure of how to respond.

"Does he?" Atlas chuckles. "I don't even know what that kid's up to these days."

"Maxim hasn't been around much lately, has he? It must be hard to see your only son so seldom, Atlas."

Penny gasps. Atlas and Maxim don't share even the slightest resemblance.

"Not at all. He turned out to be a much better person than his father, and as a parent, I couldn't be happier."

"Wait, Atlas is Maxim's father? So Maxim grew up in this cave, too?" Penny asks.

"That's right," Otra answers. "That's how I've known Maxim since we were little—and so has Doje. This place has practically been our playground since our youth. Atlas is like a father to us." Otra wraps an affectionate arm around the much smaller Atlas. "Atlas, remember how adorable Doje was? He had his peculiar way of speaking even back then."

"It's simply my way of honoring the departed. I've borne witness to many deaths since my youth, that is why . . ." Doje trails off.

"Well, this place brings back so many memories after all these years. I get nostalgic whenever I come here. When I was a kid, my mom and dad would always use me as an excuse to borrow money from others, claiming that raising me was expensive. It's not something other parents typically do. So, to play along, I would pretend I was pitiful when someone visited our home, even though I was typically in a good mood. What's ironic is that my parents never actually spent any of that money on me." Otra talks about her past as if it were no big deal.

"I'm afraid all this talk of your past out of the blue is making the young lady feel uncomfortable. Even I, in my limited understanding, know that much," Doje says, glancing at Penny.

"My, my, look at me. I'm being careless again. Forgive me, Penny. It's just that I feel closer to you ever since you visited my house."

Penny recalls Yasnoozz Otra's mansion.

"I'm so glad you've all grown up to become such great friends," Atlas says. "Maxim had to spend his childhood in the cave because of me. And Doje went through a hard time, too. His gift of seeing death brought him a lot of hardship. But in truth, life and death are never far apart." He wipes the corner of his eye with his calloused hand and looks fondly at Otra and Doje.

"It matters little to me now," Doje responds, "for this is the place where the shadows of dreamers find repose, and where our shadowed minds find solace. A tree takes time to firmly anchor its roots deep into the earth. As winter descends upon the forest without cause, suffering visits us sometimes through no fault of our own. Let us not harbor excessive sorrow for those at rest here, for in time, they shall all find tranquillity," he says calmly.

Before, Penny's steps were heavy at the thought of leaving behind their regulars at the Noctiluca Laundry. But now she finally feels relieved. Maxim, Otra and Doje, who spent their childhoods in these caves, have each forged distinct but resilient lives. The guests who are currently staying in the cave will eventually fare as well as they have. As the group stands and converses for a while, the night shadows, which have been observing them, draw closer once again—blissfully curious. Penny doesn't feel like shooing them away.

NINE

MEGA PAJAMA FESTIVAL

The heat wave has finally broken, and a cool fall breeze blows in. The first day of the Pajama Festival has dawned bright and early, and the staff members eagerly wait for their guests, fully prepared and filled with excitement.

"Now, let's open this door and let the party begin! On the count of one, two, three!"

Weather swings open the entrance. The staff marvel and exclaim at the sight. Penny stands in the doorway, overwhelmed by the scene before her: the decorations they've spent months preparing, the colorful booths, and the food trucks that have driven in from all over the country, all lining the streets in an orderly fashion.

People in bedroom slippers and sleeping socks have already filled the city. No one is dressed in their day clothes. At first, they seem to feel awkward, walking around in their pajamas, but soon, they are giggling and

having fun seeing each other in their rarely seen sleeping attire.

At first, the guests are hesitant to climb into the beds
spread out on the streets. Then, a group of middle
schoolers hop on to a white king-size bed and start a
pillow fight, which signals the beginning of the mer-
riment. Everyone grabs their family and friends and
crowds into nearby beds.

Penny is dying to put on the new pajamas she has
packed in her bag. "I can't wait for my hours to be
over. I'm so ready to toss off this apron and dash out
the door in my pajamas. Why is the time passing so
slowly today?" She sulks, standing at the front desk
with Weather.

"Tell me about it! I can't wait to get off work too and
go to the party with my kids. How about this. Why
don't you and Motail have 'a final check' on all the
booths outside? Go take a look!"

"Are you sure? Thank you, Weather!"

Weather smiles and then calls out to Motail, who is
staring longingly out of the lobby window. "Motail,
don't just loiter there. Go out with Penny and have
some fun. If you come across any broken decorations,
let me know. And check if the booths need anything."

"Perfect timing. I was just about to sneak out if you
didn't let me." Motail grins.

★ ★ ★

Penny and Motail deliberately take a long detour around the dreammakers' booths instead of heading straight to them. They stroll leisurely, taking in the lively party atmosphere. Boys and girls are reveling in the opportunity to spend all day and night with their friends, free from scolding adults. Some people seem to be from other towns, having traveled here to join the party. They stylishly sport sleep masks above their foreheads like sunglasses.

"Well, I can't stay still." Motail pulls a pair of neatly rolled sleeping socks from his pockets. He slips them on and glides past Penny on a sidewalk that has been mopped so clean it looks like he's ice-skating on it. "Penny, hurry up!"

"Be careful, Motail. You're going to hurt yourself!"

"Don't worry. The worst that can happen here is that you land on a soft bed. There are beds and blankets everywhere!"

Penny and Motail arrive at booths selling memories-themed dreams. One booth is all in pink, emanating romantic vibes. It is immediately clear whom the booth belongs to.

"Welcome, Penny and Motail! Our booth certainly stands out the most, doesn't it?" Keith Gruer looks happy to see them, nodding his shaved head. He has company—Celine Gluck and Chuck Dale. The three dreammakers have one thing in common: a natural talent for tactile sensation.

"I see the three of you have joined forces. What kind of memories inspire this dream? Does it reflect all your tastes?" Motail picks up one of their dream boxes. The wrapping paper is pale pink—almost white. Combined with the sentimental background music playing in the booth, it has a melancholy feel to it.

"The dream is called 'Memories of First Love.'"

"That doesn't sound like Gluck's cup of tea," says Motail. "She's more of an action-packed, high-stakes, fight-or-flight kind of dreammaker."

"Don't worry, I did mix in my own flavor, so you'll have a more thrilling ending than the original memory. I thought about making it a full recreation of the memory or just enhancing the faded senses, but we wanted to play to our strengths, so we put a lot of emphasis on the tactile element. I'm sure you'll feel like you're back in the moment, sensewise," Celine Gluck says confidently. She's wearing a pink T-shirt that befits the booth.

As they talk, more and more people swarm in.

"Looks like you'll be swamped with customers soon. We'll leave you to it and go check out the other booths. If there's anything we can do to help, just pop into the store and let us know." Penny steps aside to make way for the incoming crowd.

"Thanks. As you can see, we're good so far. But we'll reach out if we need anything." Chuck Dale waves them off with a charming smile.

Shortly after Penny and Motail take off, a man in his midthirties arrives at the booth.

"So my first love really appears in this dream?" he asks Chuck Dale as he points to "Memories of First Love."

"Of course. You'll be transported back to your youthful days in the dream tonight."

The man excitedly picks up the dream, and within a few moments, he falls into a deep sleep.

★ ★ ★

In his dream, the man is walking down an alley with his first love in the neighborhood where he spent his high-school years. They were inseparable during their school days, always commuting together. In the dream, he gazes at her with the same adoration as he did in the past. The night air wraps around them, and the soft glow of the streetlights illuminates their path. The alley in the dream doesn't quite match the one etched in his memory, but the discrepancies aren't distracting enough to disrupt his immersion in the dream.

They stroll side by side with their backpacks on, their

arms brushing against each other, engaging in a casual conversation filled with laughter and playful banter. Occasionally, he steals glances at her profile, mesmerized by her cuteness. The walk home from school, which typically takes a half hour, feels surprisingly short when shared with her, making him wonder if they've somehow taken a shortcut.

They find themselves in front of her house without realizing it, just as he recalls in his memory. Reluctant to part ways, they continue to wander aimlessly around the neighborhood.

As she finally heads into her house, disappointment is evident on her face, and a surge of courage overtakes him. He closes the distance between them, and just as he's about to kiss her cheek, the front door swings open, revealing her father. Panic sets in as he sees the father's face flush red. Just then, she hurriedly pushes the boy away, and he darts off.

As the boy sprints down the alley, he can feel the soles of his favorite sneakers pounding against the ground, his breath coming in gasps, his hands clutching at his school uniform top and adjusting his backpack—every sensation feels vivid and real.

In the dream, the man is unmistakably a high-school student from fifteen years ago. As he reaches the end of the alley, he murmurs to himself, "Ha . . . I should have said hello instead of running away." Even the regret he feels mirrors the man's sentiments from that bygone era.

★ ★ ★

Once he woke up, the man spent a long time reflecting on the dream. Unlike other dreams, this one, anchored in real memory, lingered. It was a delightful surprise to encounter a slice of his past that had otherwise slipped away.

What a pleasant gift. To rewind in this fast-forward life!

★ ★ ★

Over the next three days, the "Memories of First Love" booth and the "Flavors of Nostalgia" booth by Chef Grang Bong are such big hits that the department store employees have to pitch in.

The beds and bedding sponsored by the furniture stores are mostly kept clean under the watchful eye of Weather, who is in charge of the decorations, except for the antique bed in front of the shoe store, which constantly remains a mess.

"Look at that. There's a pile of grape skins and candy wrappers on the bed, and the ears of the pillows are already ripped off. If it's the Leprechauns again, I'm not going to let it pass this time."

Fuming, Penny and Motail approach the messy bed

just as the Leprechauns descend, engage in a pillow fight with teeny-weeny pillows, and quickly fly away.

The Leprechauns typically make flying dreams, but as there are no humans with actual memories of flying unaided, they have no dreams to showcase at the party. Their frustration manifests in a ruckus as they fly from bed to bed, determined to have *the wildest party ever.*

Penny shakes off the quilt and wipes down the headboard's decorative mirror with a white cloth. Motail and Penny have been walking tens of thousands of steps a day for days, diligently checking on the booths and reporting back to the department store. They are both showing signs of wear. Motail examines his jawline in one of the bed's mirrors, and his face reflects the unintended effects of their extensive walking routine.

"Penny, do I look a little sharper?" Motail asks, wearing a cheeky smile. With his newfound confidence, he strolls down the street in his fancy new silk pajamas, highly aware of all the people passing by, hopeful for a romantic encounter—but none occurs.

Meanwhile, Penny's mind is clouded with worry as the day wears on. The party is going off without a hitch, but Customers No. 330 and 620, to whom she delivered invitations at the Noctiluca Laundry, have not yet shown up. She fears that if they don't come by the end of the party, she might lose them forever.

Penny returns to the department store, passing the children jumping about, mattress springs bouncing energetically. In the lobby, distinguished guests have arrived. The legendary dreammakers Yasnoozz Otra, Doje and Babynap Rockabye are gathered, talking to Dallergut in front of a cart loaded with dream boxes.

"We had such a tight deadline, I didn't expect you to create dreams of such exceptional quality. You are all truly amazing! I owe you a debt of gratitude," Dallergut addresses all of them.

"That was ample time for me. There's a reason why I'm called a legend!" Yasnoozz Otra responds smugly, while Doje coughs in embarrassment.

"Such audacity to say that with your own mouth!"

"In this day and age, you shouldn't shy away from confidence. You have to be proud of yourself."

"I see you've found your confidence again, Otra." Dallergut smiles.

"Had Penny not sought me out that day, I'd be confined to the Noctiluca Laundry, getting drunk with Atlas and missing out on the party—which I'd probably regret deeply if I did. Thanks to you, I now have a vision for the Lives of Others series, and 'Lives of Others: The Extended Version' is in the works, so keep an eye out!"

"I'll reserve the best spot on the first-floor shelf for you."

"Thanks for having me too, Dallergut." Babynap Rockabye, her cheeks still as milky-white as an infant's, takes Dallergut's hand.

"What do you mean? I should thank *you*! I hope it wasn't too much of a burden. You came up with quite a lot of dreams. At our age, we have to be careful not to overwork ourselves."

"Actually, seeing someone around my age like Nicholas in action has me all fired up. You know, he's been in the news quite a bit this year. He still has a lot of fire in his veins, so how could I waste my time sitting still? Your offer for the festival came at just the right time, and this has been the most fun I've had in a long while."

"What kind of memory are the dreams based on?" Penny asks as she helps Dallergut unload the dream boxes from the cart to the ground.

"Why don't you take a guess?" Dallergut teases.

"I think for Doje, it must be about memories of people who have passed away, but I'm not sure about everyone else's."

"Rockabye decided to present the conception dream to parents once more. She believes it would be a heartwarming memory to relive for those with grown-up children. What could be a more emotional memory for a parent than the day they discovered they were going to become a parent?" Dallergut responds for Rockabye.

"And what about your dreams, Otra? Will they focus on other people's memories, like last time?"

"Well, that's not the kind of dream you can create in abundance. This time, it won't be from another person's perspective. You know what my other speciality is—a dream that compresses a lengthy period of time and allows you to experience it all in a single night."

The lobby of the Dallergut Dream Department Store now has a display of a series of memory-themed dreams by the legendary dreammakers. However, since the display was set up a few days after the party started, not as many customers are inside the store, so Motail takes it upon himself to attract customers, grabbing each passerby and actively selling memories.

"Listen to me, dear customers," he says, "there are three requirements for a good dream. First, it must evoke a range of emotions. Second, it must be meaningful to relive, like a movie that's worth rewatching. And third, it must be customized to the dreamer. Do you know what the one dream is that checks all these boxes?"

"What is it?"

"Memories."

He is cleverly recycling the conversation from when the staff were deciding on the theme for the party.

A steady stream of people enters the department store, not necessarily because Motail's sales tactic works, but because his over-the-top performance creates the impression that something interesting is going on in the store.

"These are memories that are too precious to let go! You'll be able to recall even the ones you've forgotten! A chance to fly back in time! Come to the Dallergut Dream Department Store right now!"

"Should we give it a try?" people ask each other.

Motail's tactics seem to work.

People start lining up to buy the dreams on display. Parents mostly buy Babynap Rockabye's dream, while older people buy Doje's dream, hoping to be reunited with someone they miss. Among the crowd, Penny finally finds the familiar faces she has been waiting for, Customers No. 330 and 620. Penny's relieved to see that they are taking Yasnoozz Otra's dream. Tonight, they'll have a wonderful dream that compresses the long days of their lives into a single movie.

***

In her dream, the retired woman who has been suffering from lethargy relives very ordinary days back in her office life.

A series of flashbacks follow—her exhausted weekday mornings and her sweet sleep-ins on weekends as a reward after a hard week, until the sound of her children calling for her jolts her and her husband awake. Rushing to get ready for work, and the faces of her neighbors greeting her when she takes the trash on her way out of the door.

There are also moments when she talks with her husband, about the kids and every household affairs, big or little, sharing the joys and sorrows of their ups and downs in life.

Life flows smoothly as they cherish both sunny and cloudy days, cook the right food for the respective occasions, and appreciate the flowers and seasonal foods that bloom and ripen. The moments of accomplishment and disappointment in her office life appear chronologically, down to the small talk she shares with her coworkers.

During the dream, Customer No. 330 finds herself back in the one-bedroom apartment where she used to live during her newlywed days, and then the two-bedroom house with a green gate they moved into after the birth of their first child. The unevenness of the ceiling and the oddly patterned tiles in the shower come alive, vivid and clear. The actual runtime of these scenes in her dream is momentary. But since every place that appears in her dream was, in fact, a cornerstone of her real life, even these brief glimpses evoke rich memories.

★ ★ ★

"Honey, I dreamed of our old house last night," the woman said when she woke up. "You know, the two-story, green-gated house where we lived on the first floor with two bedrooms, and the landlord lived on the second floor. Remember?"

The woman's husband was already up, doing his morning workout. White roots were growing out through his black-dyed hair.

"The green-gated house? Of course! I even remember the landlord's name and the phone number of the fried chicken place we used to order from on payday. I sometimes dream about the days when we lived there too. You wept when we moved out of that house. I remember asking you, 'Why are you crying when we're moving to a bigger place?' You'd shoot me a smile, but then the next moment, you'd be curled up on the floor, shedding tears again while scrubbing. I still remember our oldest son crying with you and saying, 'Mommy, don't cry.' And on moving day, the entire neighborhood could probably hear you bawling from the top of your lungs through the open gate." Her husband chuckled, sitting next to her as they reminisced about the past.

"I don't know why I cried back then. What I do remember is that, after moving everything out of the house, our voices echoed, and it sounded so unfamiliar that I hated it. I realized that all the memories in that house—eating together, chatting, putting the kids to bed, cleaning, laughing, and crying—had been packed away with our belongings. Even though it wasn't always the easiest for our family to manage there, I was really thankful for that house. I guess I cried because I felt like it had embraced us so warmly until we moved."

"I see. Do you remember the very first house we lived in, too? The tiny little room I'd been renting since I was a bachelor? It was just four walls, a ceiling and a floor, and I was embarrassed to ask you to move in with me back then. But you know what, I actually miss that place too. Remember when our blankets weren't fully dry after doing laundry even in the summer, yet we'd lie on them and talk about silly things until we fell asleep? I don't know why I remember it so fondly." The husband was more excited to share their old memories than she was.

"Wow, you remember such weird details. For me, I don't remember anything about all the fancy hotels we stayed at, well, except that the breakfast buffet was delicious. But what sticks in my mind are these ordinary days—making *kimbap* with our kids and eating *hobak jeon* for no special reason. Well, now that I think about it, we've lived a fun life."

"Yeah. We have been together so long."

"So, are you sick of me now?" the woman teased.

"Oh, you're at it again. Nonsense." Her husband

chuckled. "It's all the better—I love that we're building more memories together as time goes by." He put his hand on the back of hers and gave it a reassuring pat.

Life had always been 99.9 percent ordinary and 0.1 percent new. Now, the ordinary days had become too precious for the woman to complain about how little there was to look forward to: she found herself treasuring the cycle of seasons, the drive home after being out, the everyday meals, and the familiar faces she encountered daily.

That was when she realized that when it came to her questions—what her life had been for and where she should find her joy—she already had the answers. They'd been there all along.

In his dream, the young Customer No. 620 also finds himself immersed in memories from his past—from back when he was nineteen.

It's the end of the year, and following his disappointment with the yearly Korean SAT test, he resolves to retake it in the new year. After grappling with distress, he reaches a point where he defiantly declares, "Screw it!" In a spontaneous decision, he embarks on an overnight trip to watch the sunrise with his friends, without even packing a single sock.

He is reliving this moment in his dream.

Sitting in the cheapest seats on the train, he and his friends giggle quietly at childish jokes, trying not to distract the people around them. They try to sleep a bit until they arrive, but the acrid smell of the train makes them feel sick.

All of this feels too unbelievably real to be a dream.

The man and his friends are waiting for the sun to rise, squatting on the floor of the building they've just entered to shield themselves from the cold. They doze off, and when they wake up, it's bright out and they realize they've missed the sunrise altogether. They laugh away their disappointment, making a wish on the high sun.

In the face of his exam failure, the nineteen-year-old's wish is very clear.

"Let this time pass as if my small failure is nothing."

And when he returns home, he remembers his parents only asking him if he enjoyed his trip, their faces so warm that he could ask for nothing else.

* * *

The man awoke without remembering the entire dream, but the wish he'd made in it remained vivid, and he realized it had come true. A year of dedicated studying had led to good results and had eventually brought him to where he was today. The once-bitter experience had sculpted him into a unique individual. He desired to see what form his future self would take, even if that meant breaking apart and grinding against life. And the only way to do that was to face life head-on. The one mantra he needed at this moment was clear:

This shall pass, and it will be nothing. I'll make sure of it.

The memories that appear in dreams that week are as diverse as the attendees of the Pajama Festival. These memories linger in the recesses of each dreamer's mind, like old photo albums hidden away in a musty bookcase, waiting to be rediscovered.

Whether it's recalling a first encounter with a future best friend or reminiscing about the sunset on the way home after a taxing day, each person holds unique memories. Yet they all share something in common.

As memories transform into nostalgia, the lines between the slightest joys and sorrows begin to blur, creating a unique beauty.

"This memory is undoubtedly mine, but where was it all this time until last night?" people ask themselves.

As the attendees of the Pajama Festival awake from their dreams, they each take a moment to reflect on the past, something many of them haven't done for a long time.

★ ★ ★

It's the last day of the week-long festival. Penny has spent most of her time ensuring that all the regular customers have been taken care of, but now she's finally able to enjoy the party like everyone else.

Each day at the Dream Technology Experience Booth, a different researcher presents a new product or innovative new technology for dreammaking. Penny, with a Popsicle in her mouth, attentively listens to a young researcher, who speaks in a soft, languid voice.

"One of my recent projects focuses on what we call the *dream within a dream*, which is transitioning from one dream to the next without waking up. I'm also developing a technology that allows you to return to a pleasant dream after being interrupted, provided you go back to sleep within ten minutes. Would you like to step into the booth and try it out? It just takes thirty minutes."

"No, thanks, but I appreciate the information."

Penny shifts her attention instead to a stall selling dream catchers in various shapes. The selection is vast, with hundreds of them in all sizes, each beautifully designed to promise good dreams and ward off nightmares.

"Does the biggest dream catcher here need to be plugged into a power source?" Penny asks the vendor.

"Yes. This is the real deal. It can actually detect nightmare energy."

As soon as the vendor powers it on, the dream catcher's

feathers start spinning wildly, creating a noise reminiscent of something better suited for chasing bugs.

"Normally, it just spins around like this, but if it picks up the slightest hint of nightmare energy, it beeps loudly."

Penny, having second thoughts, considers opting for a regular dream catcher instead. Suddenly, the dream catcher stops spinning and emits an earsplitting beep.

"Hey, what's wrong?" The vendor looks around. Maxim, who happens to be walking by with Nicholas, stands frozen in place. "Oh, it must be him. I'm sorry, Maxim, but would you take a few steps back? This thing detects nightmare energy . . ."

Flustered, Maxim steps away from the dream catcher, nearly tripping over the carpet. A few people break into giggles. As Maxim stumbles, he steadies himself with his hand on the dream catcher's feathered form, causing it to howl even louder, as if in protest.

Penny feels bad seeing Maxim so uncomfortable. She doesn't want him to be treated like a nightmare just because he creates nightmares.

"How about we turn it off?!" Penny yells, but Nicholas is a step ahead of her, kicking the dream catcher so it shuts off.

"What a piece of junk," Nicholas remarks.

Maxim apologetically bows his head before hurrying away.

* * *

Penny drags her weary body back to the store. Her stomach feels like it might burst any minute from all the food she's eaten, and she's dazed by how many people she has run into.

Summer and Mogberry are still busy conducting personality tests. It proves to be so popular that even out-of-town customers are lining up, and the green-clad employees of the Civil Complaint Center are also standing in line, chatting and laughing. They look far more excited than they did at the center.

Penny weaves through the crowds until she finds Dallergut at the front desk.

"Have you taken the personality test, Dallergut? I'm guessing you're a *Third Disciple* type, right?"

"Of course I've taken it before. In fact, many times. Mogberry tested me five times, and each time I came out a different type."

"Really? That's interesting. I was a *Second Disciple* type. Probably still am. You know, I love Atlas's cave and what Maxim does and all, but is there anything distinctly good about being a *Second Disciple* type? You know, like there is for other types?"

"What makes you ask?"

"I mean, Maxim creates nightmares that bring back

past traumas, and Atlas has been living in a cave his whole life, nurturing his memories. They're both leading a life with purpose, but it just seems lonely," Penny says, remembering how Maxim reacted to the dream catcher earlier.

"I don't think their focus on the past has much to do with loneliness. I was indeed a little worried when Maxim first came out of the cave and set up the Nightmare Factory. I thought he'd be lonely by himself. But as you also saw, witnessing Nicholas and Maxim make Guilt fortune cookies this year makes me greatly relieved. It tells me he's found someone with similar goals with whom he can work. He doesn't have the space to be lonely. Neither does Atlas, who spends his time working with the Noctilucas. And I didn't feel alone this year, since you, Penny, shared the same goals as me. I think we've brought back a lot of regulars, all thanks to you. You've done very well, Penny."

"I'm glad to hear that. What a relief!"

"As for the personality test, I don't think you need to categorize your personality into these neat little boxes. It's not meant to be that way." Dallergut pulls a mint-condition case of personality test cards out of his coat pocket.

"You have one of those too, Dallergut?"

"I actually helped design them. I got sent a couple of

them as a souvenir. For something that comes as a bonus with a book purchase, they're quite impressive, aren't they? And here, look at the bottom of the case."

Dallergut turns the card case over.

Live in the present for the
happiness you have now.
Look forward to the future
for happiness yet to come,
And reflect on the past, for you only
recognize happiness after it has passed.

"This test isn't meant to find out about your unique personality. It simply reflects how you're living at the moment and the circumstances in which you find yourself. It's not surprising that the results should change every time you take the test."

Dallergut takes out a few cards from the case. They portray the Time God cradling a fragment of the present in his arms. Perhaps coincidentally, the translucent overlap of the cards seems to reflect Penny like a hazy mirror.

"I sometimes ponder whether the three disciples are not three different individuals but three different facets of the same person, evolving with time. I could say that my passage of time exists solely for me from the moment

I was born, so the Time God of my life is actually me. If I look at it that way . . . isn't it incredible to be myself?"

"Wow, I can definitely see how you could interpret it that way." Penny feels a pleasant warmth as she embraces the richness of having a present, a past and a future of her own.

"It's the same for all of us, employee or customer. There are times to live in the present, times to reflect on the past, and times to stride ahead. We all have those times, and that's why we have to wait. Because even if people don't come to us for dreams right now, there will come a time in their lives when they'll need dreams."

"Yeah. I see what you mean."

★ ★ ★

"Dallergut, we're selling out of all the dreams we've got lined up, and it's all because I've been out there working hard to get people in the door. I hope you will take this into account in my next year's salary negotiation!" Motail shouts from a distance.

"I admire Motail's tenacious spirit. I don't expect all our regulars to return thanks to this single event, though. Many of them will still be at the Civil Complaint Center and the Noctiluca Laundry. What we can do is have their dreams ready and waiting. Because—"

"Because we all have those moments, right?" Penny finishes.

Just then, a customer passes the front desk and nods farewell to Penny and Dallergut. The customer is leaving empty-handed.

"Excuse me, sir. You didn't find any dreams you liked?"

"No, actually, I felt like I'd be content sleeping without dreaming tonight." The customer chuckles sheepishly.

"I see. There are nights like that," Penny replies.

The customer stops and looks back at Penny. "I'm surprised to hear that from a store employee. I thought you were going to grab me and try to sell me a dream."

"There's no rush. I'm sure you'll visit us again." Penny's earnest smile bears a wisdom quite like Dallergut's. "Dear customer," she says, "our dream department store will always be here for you."

EPILOGUE 1

DREAMS OF THE YEAR AWARDS

After the Pajama Festival, the entire shopping district experiences an unprecedented boom. Not only the Dallergut Dream Department Store, but all the stores that participated in the festival see a noticeable increase in sales.

The most significant growth occurred at Bedtown Furniture, which produces high-end beds and bedding. Their generous sponsorship of the festival allowed people to indulge in crumbly potato chips and noodle soup on their beds. This small luxury brought great satisfaction, and the positive experiences naturally led to a fondness for Bedtown's bedding sets, resulting in a swift sellout whenever they were restocked.

Meanwhile, the buzz at the Dallergut Dream Department Store revolves around the recent surge in sales on the second floor. About three months after the festival, they have outpaced sales on the first floor.

The secret is the Imprinting Service that Vigo Myers and the second-floor staff ambitiously launched. Following the party, Myers and his team worked tirelessly to
revitalize the daily corner, which had received relatively
less attention. They came up with the idea of offering
an impromptu engraving service for customers buying
dreams. They installed a laser engraving machine, imprinting the buyer's name rather than the conventional
maker's name on a faux leather case, adding a personalized touch. Penny sees an article in *Interpretations Better
than Dreams* that says people are buying themselves a
dream marked with their name as the creator as a way to
celebrate their own birthdays.

"Dear customer, this dream is inspired by your memory, so you should be named the creator. All of us are
exceptional dreammakers in our own right, and neither the maker nor the seller can complete the dream
without you, the person who lives it every day." With
that, Myers hands over the dream box, and the customer
walks out of the store, thrilled to see their name im-
printed on the case.

"It wouldn't have been as impressive had Motail said
it. It only works because it comes from Myers, who is
utterly incapable of saying empty words." Speedo has his
own interpretation of the popularity of the second floor,
which everyone seemed to agree with, except for Mo-

tail. He seems unhappy that the popularity of the second floor means fewer products are coming to the discount section on the fifth floor.

"Cut us some slack, Myers. Sweet-talking customers into buying products is our expertise on the fifth floor."

But that is not the sole reason for the second floor's popularity. Kids who initially came to the third floor for dynamic or somewhat disturbing dreams were often dragged by their parents to the second floor, where the products are certified to contain only harmless ingredients.

"Mom, please, can I have the dream I want?"

"Just try out one dream I choose for you, honey. You've already picked out a week's worth of dreams."

★ ★ ★

The trend for the second floor continues through the end of the year. Even as people gather at the Dallergut Dream Department Store to watch the Year-End Awards on the big screen, Vigo Myers and the second-floor Memories section are still a hot topic.

"I caught Vigo Myers grin like a kid printing out his name all over the creator sections on the dream boxes. I bet the Imprinting Service in the Memories section was his way of making himself feel like a dreammaker."

The Leprechauns, perched on the chairbacks like

sparrows, chirp away. Penny, sitting nearby, glares at them as coldly as she can. She's got to know Myers quite well this year, and doesn't like it when people gossip about him.

Word seems to have spread that the Dallergut Dream Department Store is the best place to watch the Year-End Awards show, and viewers flood the lobby, including some Noctilucas and a few other dreammakers who are rarely seen in the shopping district.

Customers and animals passing by on the street crowd in front of the department store, peering inside.

"Please come in and join us if you'd like," Dallergut encourages them. It is obvious that there aren't enough chairs for everyone, but the shrewd Dallergut calls out with one quick clap. "How about we push the chairs aside and sit on the floor today? Luckily, we have plenty of mats."

As soon as he finishes his sentence, the staff members move in unison, creating more seating space. Weather dims the lights and places leftover candles from the pajama party around the room. It creates a cozier mood, and the chatter quiets. Penny sits down on a mat with Assam and stretches her feet.

Out of nowhere, an orange tabby cat crawls on to Assam's lap.

"You sure know the comfiest spot."

Penny watches as Dallergut fumbles with the cables to the beam projector. Eventually he manages to get them connected, and the awards show appears on the giant screen.

"Dallergut, here's an empty space," calls Weather. "Come!"

Dallergut sits on the same mat with Weather and, surprisingly, Doje and Yasnoozz Otra. Doje looks as stoic as a rock. It's quite possible that Otra forced him to join her.

Speedo squeezes in beside them. "Hey, Doje, where do you buy your clothes? If you let down that high bun, will your hair be long like mine? Why do you always wear the same color? I also like to wear the same things over and over. I think we have a lot in common."

"Nothing about my attire is strategic. I simply choose what appeals to me . . ."

Penny watches Doje shift on his mat to make sure Speedo can't sit next to him.

Doje and Yasnoozz Otra are not the only celebrities sitting nearby. Behind Penny and Assam, Kick Slumber sits with Animora Bancho, who creates dreams for animals. Assam, a longtime admirer of Kick Slumber, pretends to focus on Bancho, who's rolling around with his dogs on the floor. But all the while he's discreetly stealing glances at Kick Slumber.

"Oh my god, look at all the celebrities here! This place feels more like the awards show than what's on the screen, Penny."

"Relax, Assam."

Assam takes a deep breath and pets the cat in his lap. "How can I relax when I know who's sitting behind me?"

"I know. I understand."

Penny wonders why Kick Slumber and Animora Bancho are here and not at the awards ceremony. Bancho won the Bestseller category last year, and Kick Slumber won the Grand Prix.

"Everyone, look at the screen! Myers is about to appear." The staff from the second floor get excited.

The awards show is in full swing. The host is about to announce the winner of the Bestseller.

"And at last, the winner for the Bestseller category is 'Memories' from the Dallergut Dream Department Store! We could not identify the dreammaker because each memory dream is created by the dreamer themselves. But Vigo Myers, the manager of the second floor, will accept the award on their behalf."

This outcome wasn't unexpected given their remarkable sales. People congratulate the second-floor staff, shouting and cheering. On the screen, Myers is in the same suit he always wears to the store, except he now has a bow tie. He looks nervous, and after accepting the award, he walks right off the stage without saying a word, only to be grabbed by the host and dragged back toward the microphone.

"You can't just leave! Give us a few words of acceptance, please! Okay, here you go, I'm going to give you the microphone again, Mr. Vigo Myers. You're nervous, I know. Let's give him a round of applause, everyone!"

Myers stands at the center of the stage, fiddling with his mustache as he thinks for a moment about what to say.

"It's not technically my award, so . . . I'm embarrassed to say it, but it's been a dream of mine to win an award at the Dream of the Year Awards. I suppose living long enough to see this day makes it all worthwhile. I hope you'll continue to love both our ordinary and extraordinary dreams on the second floor of the Dallergut Dream Department Store. Um . . . Can I go now?" With that, Myers quickly walks off the stage.

"It's a shame he's so blunt, even in his acceptance speech! But he seems to be in a much better mood than usual. I can tell," Mogberry says as she sips her nonalcoholic beer. She strokes Bancho's dogs as she walks over and crouches on Kick Slumber's mat.

"You two don't have any nominations for this year's awards? Must be disappointing," Mogberry says, looking at Slumber and Bancho.

"We'll get the Grand Prix next year." Slumber's response catches everyone by surprise.

"*We*? Are you two making a new dream together?" asks Penny, turning to face him.

"Yes. We're working on a new project. Isn't that right, Bancho?"

"Yeah, I'm so honored. Slumber makes dreams for people to experience what it feels like to be a certain animal, and I create dreams purely for animal customers from their perspective. And we both realized there's a dream that would be the perfect combination."

"And what kind of dream is that?"

"Penny, do you know of any animals that have never lived as animals?"

"Animals but not animals . . . What? I mean, why do people love quizzing me?"

"Aha, sorry for the random question. We're making a dream for our animal friends confined in the zoo, hoping they can spend at least a third of their lives where they're supposed to be."

"Wow, I never thought it was possible to create a dream like that! When it's released, no one should dare wake the sleeping animals at the zoo by knocking on the glass of their enclosures. It would be a shame if they woke up from such dreams." Penny is excited about the idea for this new product coming to the fourth floor next year.

★ ★ ★

The awards ceremony has now come down to the announcement of the Grand Prix of the Year, and for some reason, there is no suspense. Everyone seems to know who the Grand Prix winner will be.

"Assam, what dream do you think will win the Grand Prix?"

"Have you not heard the rumor?"

"What rumor?"

"People keep saying that Babynap Rockabye is fully back to her prime. That means she's got no opponent."

As soon as Assam responds, the host announces the winner.

"This year's Grand Prix goes to . . . Babynap Rockabye's 'Redreaming Conception Dreams'!"

Amid thunderous applause, Babynap Rockabye, elegantly attired, strides onto the stage flanked by her bodyguards.

"At the memory-themed Pajama Festival, Babynap Rockabye shared tender conception dreams for parents, revisiting the emotion of having a child for the first time. Described as a phenomenal experience, this dream allowed parents to relive the excitement of welcoming a new life. Now, let's hear more from the winner herself."

Babynap Rockabye comes onstage and adjusts the microphone to match her short height.

"I'm sorry to say, this old lady takes another Grand Prix. I guess that means I've still got some good years left in me. Looking back on the production of this dream brought back a flood of emotions, taking me back to the days when I saw those two lines on my pregnancy test and my first ultrasound picture. How amazing would it be to treat everyone around us with the same excitement as when we first meet them! I hope I can continue to work with the same excitement I had when I first started this job. To all you older dreammakers out there, I want to challenge you to keep up with me!"

That is when the camera catches Nicholas in the audience, who rises and gives a standing ovation to Rockabye. He rarely attends the awards shows, but this year, he's present, and dressed to the nines. And every time Nicholas is on screen, Maxim, who is sitting next to him, is seen blushing.

"I see Lady Rockabye is still well in her prime." Doje claps admiringly.

"Good, I guess it's not too late for me either! I'll have to aim for the Grand Prix next year with 'The Lives of Others: The Complete Edition'!" Otra says, straightening her coat collar.

The clock approaches midnight. As Penny waits for the countdown, she silently prays that in the coming year, she can approach her job with the same passion that she had when she first started, just as Babynap Rockabye said. And that in the next year, and the ones that follow, she will continue to watch the Year-End Awards show with everyone here at the Dallergut Department Store.

EPILOGUE 2

MAXIM AND THE DREAM CATCHER

The holidays are over, and a new year has begun. The temperature has dropped, and today it's sleeting. Penny takes off her furry mittens. They're soaked from the snow. Her fingertips are numb, and all she wants is to reach her destination.

Penny waddles through the snow, struggling to carry a paper bag almost as big as she is. The fragile handles have long since snapped under the weight of the bag's contents.

Penny has been worrying that what she is about to do will come off as nosy, but before she knows it, she arrives in front of her destination: Maxim's Nightmare Factory. There are piles of frozen leaves, leftover from fall, and mounds of unused items lying around. The only thing that has changed is the window, which is now draped in dark gray curtains, unlike the first time she visited when they were pitch-black. Penny stands at the top of the stairs, but she can't bring herself to knock. She's still thinking of the words she wants to say to Maxim when the door swings open.

"Penny, what are you doing here . . . ?"

Maxim, dressed in a gray sweater knitted with coarse yarn, stands there with a surprised look on his face.

"Oh, hi."

"Why didn't you knock? It's cold outside. Come on in."

"Oh, yes, it's been pretty chilly these days, huh? Actually, it's not chilly, it's freezing. And snowing . . . I guess it's because it's winter, and it's always cold in winter. Look, I'm not going to come inside, I'm just here to give you this." After rambling for a while, Penny extends the paper bag she's been awkwardly lugging around.

"I'm not sure what this is, but I can't just let you freeze out here, so come on in," says Maxim. "I insist."

If they keep standing like this, both Maxim and Penny will turn into snowmen. The snow is getting thicker and thicker under Maxim's feet. Regretting her decision to visit, Penny awkwardly steps into Maxim's Nightmare Factory.

The studio looks more complex than it did the last time Penny visited with Dallergut. New shelves have been added to store more dream ingredients, with more hanging in big nets from the hooks below. On the worktable, small background chunks in various colors look like miniplanets as they sleep quietly in their clear, unopened cases.

"Please have a seat there. I'll make you some hot tea." Maxim gestures to the worktable and chair. While he brews the tea, Penny thinks long and hard about whether or not she should take out the item from the paper bag.

"Here you go. This is my favorite herbal tea to drink when I work. It has no special effects, but it has a great aroma. By the way, what brings you here? I don't suppose the staff at the Dream Department Store are going around personally greeting all the dreammakers for the New Year. You guys are busy people. I'm surprised that you came to see me on your own."

Penny glances at Maxim, who is looking at her kindly, and decides to stop beating around the bush.

"Please don't laugh or make fun of me." She takes a deep breath and pulls something out of her paper bag. It is a large round hoop with strings of woven elements dangling from it.

"Is this a dream catcher?"

"Yes, it is!"

Penny is overjoyed that Maxim recognizes it right away, smiling with glee. She made the dream catcher herself and has been reluctant to show it to Maxim because of how sloppily it turned out. She is greatly relieved that he can identify what it is.

"Did you make this yourself, Penny?"

"I mean, who would sell a dream catcher as messy as this?" Penny shrugs with a sheepish smile, and shows Maxim the details of the ornaments she has haphazardly strung to the dream catcher. A circular ring made of macramé is overstuffed with feathers, beads and shells, which she'd thrown on to cover up her poor knotting skills. She imagines that anyone who sees it will feel sorry for the hoop, which barely holds the dangling ornaments together.

"It's beautiful." Maxim stares in genuine awe.

Penny is surprised. She was expecting he'd make fun of it.

"But why are you giving this to me? You made it by hand. It must be special."

Maxim hits her with the question she's been dreading. She has no idea how to respond. And this is why she has spent days debating whether or not to visit his studio.

"It doesn't really mean anything. Well, it does mean something, but there's no pressure. It's just that, at the pajama party . . . It was probably the last day, when I saw you startled by the dream catcher, and I felt bad. So, I made one that has no real function . . . Which may be an issue, because it's a dream catcher that doesn't look like or function like a dream catcher. But at least you might feel safe with this one, so . . ."

Penny remembers the way the electronic dream catcher blared loudly, sensing Maxim's nightmare energy, and making him panic.

Maxim says nothing.

"Um, sorry if I made you feel uncomfortable, I'll just take it back. I just . . ." Penny stammers, and Maxim waves his hands.

"No! I just don't know what to say in a situation like this. I've never been so happy. How do you express your emotions when you're beyond ecstatic?" Maxim asks in a serious tone.

"Oh. I wasn't expecting something that dramatic, but . . . So you *do* like the gift? I'm glad."

Penny picks up the dream catcher and looks around the room.

"Let's see, I think this would be a nice spot to hang it." She points to one of the hooks beneath the high shelves, facing the gray blackout curtains. "So, if we hang it like this . . . This looks nice! Hey, Maxim. Come over here and take a look."

Maxim joins Penny, standing with his back to the window. Inside the circle of the dream catcher, his workspace comes into view.

"Now all the dreams you create here will filter through this dream catcher and go out into the world as wonderful, positive dreams."

"Wow . . . This is amazing."

Maxim stands slouching, staring at the dream catcher. The room is dead silent. Penny runs out of words. She thinks it was rash for her to come here alone.

Maxim remains as motionless as a still image, showing no signs of initiating further conversation. It appears that Penny must decide whether to continue the conversation, or toss out a parting comment like, "Great talk!"

Penny opens her mouth to say something, when, to her surprise, Maxim breaks the long silence.

"Penny, are you happy working at the dream department store?"

"What? Why do you ask . . . ?"

"I'm curious. I want to know."

"Why, yes. I'm loving it. Sure, it's tiring and a pain sometimes. But I'm glad that I get to be around and observe so many people. What about you, Maxim? Do you like being a dreammaker? Oh, I guess the answer is a given. I heard from Atlas at the Noctiluca Laundry about how hard you worked to get out of the cave and become a dreammaker all by yourself, and that must be because you love the job."

"My father must have told you. It's embarrassing, but yes, you're right. Creating dreams is such a fascinating job."

"Then, let me change the question. What's been your favorite moment since you left the cave?"

"Right now," Maxim answers right away. "This is my favorite moment."

Speechless, Penny struggles to gulp down her still-hot tea.

"Actually, Penny. I just thought of an idea of how to express this ecstatic moment."

"Yeah? What's that?"

"Well, I guess it's a very *Second Disciple* thing to say."

"What is it?"

"Today, I've made a memory that I'll cherish for the rest of my life. In the future when I have a good dream, the background will always be this space where we're sitting together."

Penny can't recall the last time she heard something that made her blush so much. How does he have the nerve to say those words? But when she compares her back-to-back late nights building the dream catcher with Maxim's endearing words, she knows which one wins. And knowing the answer, she bursts out chuckling.

Just then, the dream catcher hanging on the shelf hook spins in midair. The dangling ornaments clink against each other, a sound effect that complements their shy laughter quite nicely.

★ ★ ★ ★ ★

TRANSLATOR'S NOTE

I know you can't believe this is the end of the story, and that you'd rather be reading more about Penny and Maxim than my Translator's Note. Believe me, no one wishes for that more than I do.

In fact, the story is just beginning, because Miye Lee has now unlocked a whole new dream world for us to explore while we sleep. Since translating the duology, I've been dreaming more—and remembering my dreams more—since I have begun a new habit of writing dream journals. If I dream of a fantastical landscape that I'm certain was crafted by Wawa Sleepland, I can't bear to forget it so I write it down. And when I wake up from a nightmare, I find myself not trembling in fear, but smiling, thinking of how Maxim's studio is now ever-so-slightly brighter thanks to Penny's handmade dream catcher.

Thank you, Miye, for inviting us all into a dream world we didn't know existed within us. I feel incredibly honored to help share this world with English readers and it wouldn't have been possible without the immense help and support of my editors, Areen Ali and John Glynn. And a special thank you to my beta reader Hyeyoung, who challenges me for the title of Dallergut's biggest fan.

I also want to thank all the readers who have so warmly welcomed this dream world. It was truly rewarding to see the love for the first book of the duology, not just from readers but also from booksellers. I envision a beautiful parallel between dream stores and bookstores, where countless Dallerguts, Weathers and Pennys carefully display and sell books, much like dreams, with an abundance of love and care.

While the duology ends here for now, this is not the end of the Dallergut Dream Department Store. Who knows? Maybe one day we'll see the store in a different medium, or maybe there will be a prequel about Dallergut's younger days. You see, I'm the most hopeful fan, and saying goodbye to Dallergut's wonderful store is never an option for me.

So I won't say goodbye to you either, because I will see you at the Dallergut Dream Department Store tonight.

Sweet dreams,
Sandy Joosun Lee